ETERNAL

WRITTEN BY DAVID GERE

Printed in the United States of America

First printing, 2016

ISBN: 0692765204
ISBN:9780692765203
Library of Congress Control Number: 2016913092
David Dorfmeier, Paso Robles, CALIFORNIA

CONTENTS

This book is dedicated to those, who like me, never stopped believing in it.
And to my wife, without you, this story never would have been completed.

PROLOGUE

I have seen many things. What I'm going to share with you now, I once wrestled with for some time, but no longer. It is not just a story, as I had once thought, but a truth thousands of years old.....

No one runs from who they are forever! ---- Eric Richards

CALLED OUT

Germany
1944

As the wheels settled on the tarmac, I turned away from the briefing Major Bergen had sent forward when he'd called me from the front lines. I looked out at the city, for a moment it looked different from the movie reels five years prior. The Major greeted me in a shiny black sedan, "Greetings Fredric, my old friend!"

His associate and driver, Stulgard, shook my hand as I entered the sedan. In his usual manor, Bergen wasted no time in explaining the details of that evening and the next day.

"The meeting will take place at noon. No one else aside from the three of us will be in attendance. You will salute him and not look the Fuhrer directly in the eyes by any means," he said in his usual deep voice.

I could see the stress practically written out upon his forehead with every drop of sweat steeping slowly. My attention had been distracted only by the nervous twitch he usually hides from his men in public.

Maybe that twitch, which came from days, months, even years in battle, wouldn't have been noticeable, except he could barely light a cigarette without it dancing around his fingers. Honestly, I felt bad for my friend, the war had not been kind to him. He was no longer the man that had commanded so many in battle before that day. Only a shell of that person remained. I wondered how he would function in a different type of life.

Bergen jolted up in his seat after giving the driver directions to the hotel we'd be staying at that night.

"This will change everything you know!" His expression gleamed, I had not seen him that excited as long as I'd known the man.

I had no idea what he meant by that remark.

"Fredric," he said in only a slight whisper, he rarely called me by my first name.

"It's almost over you know, not that I care anymore which way things go!" this had surprised me, the major tugged on my shoulder.

"You know how I've given everything to this cause. It's obvious I'll never see that life they promised me. 'For your troubles, we'll give you a house and land,'" he'd stopped only a second to chuckle at the thought of being a man who could even enjoy all that, without his wife and kids, who'd left him a year before.

I didn't have time to ask him how that meeting would change everything, but I would find out for myself. And in as little as four days, my entire life would never be the same.

Before I could ask, we had arrived at the most beautiful hotel in all of Berlin, or all of Germany for that matter.

He went on to say, " No expense has been spared for us my boy, great views and great service," he grinned and I knew he meant anything including the company of a lady could be mine on the house.

Of course he also knew I was married and maybe that was the reason for that half smile in the first place.

"Well this is our stop, see you in the morning and don't stay up too late my boy," he'd given me a wink before heading up the stairs ahead of me, I just shook my head as usual.

"I guess I'll see you later, Sir. We'll make a little bit of history and I can finally clear my debt and go home some kind of hero in the process".

"Maybe," he said as the glass door closed behind him.

No one else knew Hitler would be in town. Of course, secrecy was also a priority for the man. As the bell hop opened the doors, I walked through, knowing then that Bergen was not lying when he said this place was amazing!

It was truly dazzling. No wonder Adolf would insist on stay in such a place from time to time.

Mother of pearl and gold inlay accentuated marble counter tops and pillar-lined stair cases. One could not help but notice the oak hand rail that was also carved by hand, showing some serious craftsmanship. The staircase wrapped around seemingly the entire entrance.

I stopped a man walking by to ask if the hotel had always been this busy, "As long as I can remember," he replied

I caught myself in that moment looking like some kind of tourist lost in the scenery. It was then that an absolutely stunning dark haired woman no older than twenty-four approached me. She had obviously been busy herself.

"Must be the uniform," I thought to myself.

"Can I have someone grab your things, Sir?" I looked at her for a moment before speaking.

"No, that's fine," I told her with a smile.

She took her hands off the few bags I was already carrying.

"Well at least let me show you to your room, it's on the fourth floor."

She then guided me toward the elevator and stopped as we waited for it to return to the level we were on.

She stared at me with one of those looks, "You have any plans tonight? Maybe going out to the bars? You may have seen the one across the street, most go over there."

"I think I'll be going to bed early, but thank you for the offer."

I paused for a moment, then continued, "Don't you need to know my name for the room?"

She chuckled, "Your friend, Major Bergen, called ahead to give me your name and description."

"Here we are," she pointed to the hallway on the left, "Your room is 135B, all the way at the end of the hall. It's one of our four suites!"

As I walked down the hallway, I laughed to myself for a moment, thinking it must have been Major Bergen joking with me. That thought was soon interrupted, as I heard her shout down the hall, "Don't forget, room service is just a phone call away."

I shut the door as quickly as I could, thinking she'd find another reason to bother me. I was tired that night, but would not see any sleep for a while.

I had gotten no further than five steps when I heard a noise coming from the bathroom. I drew my Luger from its holster. If someone was here to kill me, I wasn't about to be caught off guard and be taken out like that. I heard a soft voice singing, one that sounded strangely familiar, through the rushing water of the shower.

"Hun, is that you?"

As I heard the question clear as day, I wondered how it could be her. A lump formed in the back of my throat. The words almost didn't come out as I struggled to bring them forward. My mouth opened to deliver only a whisper, "Maria?"

No word in reply. She goes back to singing, as the beautiful tone strikes softly against the tiles in the bathroom.

She sang as though only angels could hear the sound. I knew then without a doubt it was my wife, whom I had not seen in almost two years. All I could think of in that moment was 'how'. How did she know where I was and why had she come to see me? Not that I wasn't happy to see her, but her presence raised some serious questions. Was she in trouble? Or was she compromising my mission by even being at the hotel? It made me angry at first, but at the same time, I missed her. A year had already gone by since I left to fly missions in Russia.

Quickly, I decided to put my pistol away once I realized there was no real threat. The door was ajar, so I walked in and tried not to startle her.

"My dear, your voice is still as unhindered as the day we first met."

She instantly shouted and jumped as she turn around naked in the shower. She hadn't heard me at all.

"Fredric! God, you scared me!" she exclaimed, covering herself up with her arms and hands clinched together.

"Sorry babe, guess you didn't hear me."

Then she gave me a glare, "Could you grab me a towel?"

I laughed and handed the towel over.

"You don't really need it. I'll just be taking it off again in a minute."

She shot me another look and a smile.

"Well that's presuming a lot for a husband I haven't seen in a year."

Maria turned off the shower and stepped out, wrapped in a towel. She reached out and caressed the stubble on my haggard face, "I've missed you," she said softly.

"I've missed you too."

"I began to think I'd never see you again," she said as her eyes started to well up with tears.

Then out of nowhere, she smacked me right across the face.

"Not one word!" the anger overtaking her more gentle side.

"A year and I heard nothing from you! I didn't know if you were alive or dead!" Before Maria could hit me again I grabbed her wrist.

"Look, I'm sorry. I couldn't risk contacting you, especially after they moved me to these missions. I have been flying a lot lately."

She had known it would be like this, all the secrecy. But that knowledge, though true, did not lessen the hurt we both felt.

I held her by the waist, "I promise not a day has passed that I didn't think of every moment we had shared together before I left."

A single tear fell. I wiped it from her cheek as she smiled.

"How about this, we put the past behind us. You're here now, that's all that matters to me," she said softly.

With that, I held her even closer, putting an entire year worth of love into a single kiss. I took the white towel off her head unveiling her still glowing long blonde hair.

"Is it me, or have you gotten even more beautiful?" I remarked, as the towel hit the floor next to her feet, followed by the other towel wrapped around her body.

My hands caressed her shoulders as if they were drawn to them, then moved slowly down her waist.

"Apology accepted," she whispered between kisses.

"You're still tough on the outside, but beyond that, you're nothing but a softy," she commented as she unbuttoned my uniform.

Maria's deep blue eyes said only one thing. This was a look I had missed for so long, a simple gaze meaning nothing less than total love.

Gently, I moved her to the next room. I could not end what had begun nor would I ever want to. But the truth we both denied in that moment was the hurt that would come back in the morning. I would leave once again. The only difference being it was my last mission, my final flight in a year long life of secrets and lies. A peace came over me knowing that the war would be over soon. I knew that I would go home safely to my wife, set to make a new life with her far from Germany. We would live like royalty on the money I was promised.

All I could think about was how much I loved Maria and how I hoped she knew I had done everything for her. How I could not wait to have children and grow old in a beautiful home with her. One week and this nightmare would be over forever. I chose to stop thinking about what I could not change, but rather take in the moment of making love to my wife.

"I've never slept so well in my life," Maria remarked, with one hand on my chest and the rest of us wrapped up in the covers.

"Me either," I said, taking a moment to stretch and give her one more kiss.

Rumbles from her stomach had broken the silence and the rays from the sun breaking through the curtains would not let us sleep longer anyway.

"Breakfast, beautiful?"

Maria's stomach already confirmed my thoughts.

"Oh yes, I could eat everything they've got!" she said elated at the thought of smoked bacon and eggs.

"I'll call room service and charge it."

Maria jumped up and ran across the room naked to get a robe, then picked up the phone to order.

"Get up lazy bones!" she laughed and I just smiled.

"Okay, okay, I'm getting up. Cigarette and coffee first?"

With a nod she agreed and passed me one. After the smoke and coffee, I decided not to waste any more time and jumped in the shower. I had figured it would take at least thirty minutes for breakfast.

"Alright Maria, I'll be in the shower!"

As I was getting into the shower, there was a knock at the door.

"Room service," the man said, as Maria opened the door.

What she didn't realize was that I had left the shower going but never stepped in. I slowly crept to the bathroom door to see if I could hear anything. There was no way our food had been cooked already. The truth was I didn't want to believe the unthinkable, but anything was possible. Even Maria could betray me because of this mission.

As I listened in, I could hear everything that they were saying.

"Is everything okay?" the bellhop muttered.

"Yes," my wife replied.

"Does your husband, suspect anything is going on?"

"No, I have taken care of any suspicions. He trusts me completely."

I moved out of the bathroom, inching my way along the wall so I could get a look at who Maria was talking to. I saw the man dressed as a bellhop, but his hat kept me from seeing his face. Just then, I saw the man give Maria an envelope.

"They will call and update you of our progress in four days."

Maria tucked the envelope in a drawer next to the door. The voice sounded familiar to me. I was still too far away though to make out everything and it didn't help that the man was whispering.

"Kevin, before you leave, you promise me one thing. Be careful and you make sure he doesn't get hurt!"

The man gave Maria a hug and left, closing the door behind him.

Quickly, without making a sound, I crawled back into the shower and soaped up really fast. I rinsed off and got out of the shower, making it look like I had been there the whole time. Maria stepped into the doorway as I was drying my hair. She showed no emotion at all, as if that conversation had not happened. I had no idea what she was up to. The only thing I could do was hope, hope I was wrong about the conclusion forming in my head.

LAST MISSION

"**F**redric, what shall we do after breakfast?" Maria said as she wrapped her arms around my waist.

"Well, I do have a couple hours before I have to leave. There's a pub just down the block."

We both knew it was a bit too early for a drink, but a little pool or some dancing would be nice.

It was a smoke-filled, turn of the century, rustic, average-sized pub. A few people were sitting at the bar. Another soldier sat in a booth by himself, looking down at his glass and back to his watch, is if he was waiting for someone or something. The others, even at ten in the morning, looked as though they were ready to drink any thoughts of the war away. A few more guys walked in from the back room with their pool sticks in hand, as if they had a full day ahead of them, taking money from suckers willing to part with it.

"Things sure kick off early around here don't they?" I said starring, but not too intently, at the men pulling out balls from the pool table and racking them up to practice.

"They sure do! That's why people like my place. I start serving at ten, well before anyone else in Berlin," said the bartender proudly.

He motioned to me to see if we'd like anything. I waved him off.

"Just two coffees," I said and motioned to the record player.

"Play anything you want," said the man, pouring fresh brewed coffee into our mugs.

Maria shuffled through a stack of records, then finally chose one and placed it on the player. A soft, gentle, bluesy tune was perfect.

"Shall we dance?" she asked, twirling her skirt while taking my hand.

That was a beautiful moment. While we danced slowly, Maria's hand curled in mine and her chin rested on my shoulder, making her blonde hair tickle my cheek. I knew it was an attempt to hold on to each moment we had left. The truth was, that moment on the dance floor only magnified the fear of possible changes in front of me.

I could not speak of the fear I had in my heart concerning the mission in front of me, or the doubt I had about what I overheard back at the hotel. Maria could not possibly know that I had listened in on her conversation. Was my love for Maria misplaced? Was the long distance and our time apart too much for our love?

I did not let my thoughts show and hid them down deep inside, hoping against all hope that I was reading into this too much.

All that was left to do was trust in our love. It had been the hope of seeing her beautiful face that kept me safe for the past year.

"No matter what happens and how things might change Fredric, just know that I love you!"

I couldn't respond right away and just held her face in the palm of my hand as the song ended.

"I love you too. I know I don't deserve you or anything good in this life after what I've done," I said, my voice shaking.

She didn't bother to ask what I meant. Someday, I knew I'd tell her when all was said and done. War was a strange beast, taking everything except for what was pure, and that was our love.

The moment we could not slow down had arrived, and it was time for us to go our separate ways.

"I have to go. I love you."

I held my wife's face softly in my hands. There was no telling if that would be the last time. My finger brushed through her golden hair and I looked into those deep blue eyes. Still, I knew one truth for sure, running away from what had to be done was not the answer.

Maria pulled my hand toward her lips and kissed it, "When you start to worry, just remember right now."

I looked around and smiled, "Except of course the thick smoke and strange characters!"

She started laughing instantly. After a few more kisses and a passionate embrace, I headed out the door.

We stopped at some kind of ammunition bunker after an hour long country drive. Fellow soldiers were posted at every point for obvious reasons. Once we got into the place, there was no other way in or out. There was no light from the outside, making the bunker completely secure. The only light source was from a single lamp in the center of the bunker. It was just bright enough to illuminate two body guards on each side of a figure, sitting ominous on a throne.

Standing in that place, I remembered what Bergen had said, "We are all marked men. After this, none of us will come back without total success in this mission."

Remembering where I was and who I was standing before, I then thought of another Bergen quote, "Whatever you do Fredric, don't look him straight in the eyes! It's about respect!"

Hitler sat in his chair looking down at his hands as if to examine the skin and how it had aged so quickly. He sat that way for a moment, then grabbed a small cigar box from his jacket and offered me one. I obliged. Saying 'no' to this man was not an option.

"Do you think a man can be trusted?" he asked, only glancing up for a moment.

I thought carefully about how to respond to his question.

"Yes, I believe some, maybe a few men can be trusted, sir."

I knew right then what the next words out of his mouth would be: Was I a man that could be trusted?

He did not ask me this, only paused as if the question and the answer were implied. "You must do this, if not for your country, then do it for me."

I sensed an urgency in his voice as if it were the last hope for Germany.

He continued, "You must not fail! If you fail, everything you hold dear will be gone, I promise you that!"

Then Adolf looked directly at me and grabbed my hand, "If you prove my trust to be misplaced, you will hang alongside anyone you care about. You are known, Fredric, for your abilities in the sky. For this reason, you and your co-pilot, Vasyl, were chosen for your courage and quick thinking even under fire!"

He opened a chest sitting on the other side of his chair slowly and moved it under the light.

"Succeed, and you will never again have need for anything as long as you live!"

The chest was filled to the hilt with gold bars stamped with the Nazi's party seal. I had never laid eyes on so much gold in all my life, or any gold for that matter.

"It will be sent to you, anywhere you desire to call home".

The mission was a somewhat simple journey down to Africa. We would fly from there in the blanket of night. The quicker route was over Russia, but the risk of being spotted was too great. We would be handed our prototype jet planes, which were called HE178's. I was in the test flights and she was an amazing piece of machinery.

Striking a deal with Japan, we would turn the tides and ensure Germany's ultimate victory. How could America stand against such technology on two fronts? It had been the biggest and most important mission given to anyone we knew of. It would also be our last. The only issue that arose with the mission was that we would be risking our lives to refuel over the Atlantic, then take just enough time to eat and sleep in Brazil. In order to conserve fuel, we were only fitted with twin machine gun turrets. The final armaments would be fitted in Japan to display for them the capabilities of the HE178.

The time had come quickly. We'd slept as much as we could, not knowing how long it would be before we could sleep again. It would have been nice to see more scenery, I'd never been to Africa. As I made my way toward the primitive outpost hanger bay, my jet fighter looked amazing. I thought to myself, only briefly, how much of a shame it was that no one else even knew they existed.

How I'd wished Maria could have been there to see it. Night had just fallen and it was time.

"She's ready for you, sir!"

I climbed in and placed a picture of Maria above the instrument panel, then kissed it before continuing.

"Counting off...3...2...1! Engines spinning! Raise throttle!"

"Raising throttle and removing blocks! Good luck, Sir!" the attendant yelled.

The boys back at camp would be jealous, especially Bergen, no doubt!

It was decided that we should leave separately to avoid detection. A single fighter is less noticeable than two. My best friend and wing man, Vasyl, had left before me. It was to take eight hours, according to Bergen's briefing, which I had read on the plane ride into Germany days earlier.

We would meet at the marker for refueling about half way to Brazil, where a fuel tanker would be waiting. Arrangements had already been made for our return by the Japanese. It was simply up to us to make sure the planes made it.

Then, the few men who'd been standing guard over the planes shouted, "FOR FUTURE GLORY! FOR GERMANY!"

Their words echoed in my head as I lifted off the tarmac. I could hardly believe that in a few short days I'd finally be done with my last mission and be a very wealthy and happy man.

I had never flown in the dark during the test flights, which proved to be a bit of a challenge. Dawn approached by the time I reached the marker. A contraption was made specifically for our jets to ensure that refueling would not pose any issues. A large floating tanker, just big enough to carry the fuel and land our jets, was fitted to float up to the surface above one of our subs.

I called Vasyl over the radio when I arrived at the tanker, "Crow to Seagull, come in Seagull! Reaching marker, need to land down on the platform!"

The platform was like a separate piece attached on the other side of the tanker. The length of which was as long as the sub, but extremely narrow, barely wide enough for my landing gear. Once sufficient time for us to refuel had passed it would be destroyed.

"Seagull do you copy? This is Crow. Very foggy, visibility is about half a kilometer. What is your position to the marker?"

DAVID GERE

There was still no answer and it made me very nervous. Vasyl should have been there before me, at least within fifteen to twenty minutes. The fueling station was the only thing that could be seen, due to its reflective paint covering the landing strip. There was no more time to be wasted in the air, so I landed, intent on refueling.

"Hey, buddy!" a shout came over the radio as Vasyl's plane quickly passed overhead.

"Been hanging around here for about ten minutes, flying in circles!" he continued and I was glad to see my old friend, not only safe but in good spirits.

We took the time to take a leak in the ocean after refueling and then it was back in the air again. We had about seven hours left before we would reach Brazil, where we would receive our final instructions and earn a good night's worth of sleep. From there, the planes would be covered and transported by boat, disguised as American vessels, south the rest of the way. We would be accompanying them for demonstration purposes.

The time passed quickly. I don't know why, maybe because of so many things racing around in my mind. Land could be seen in the distance, it was Brazil at last. We'd both been very tired and continued to talk to one another just stay awake.

"Fredric, how long have we been friends?" Vasyl asked

"Since that party four years ago. Yeah, same night that guy was shouting about the cause and how we should join," I responded with nostalgia more than anything else.

"If you hadn't backed me up, that girl would have married a loser," I laughed, remembering how we took out three of that man's friends when they tried to put us down.

While thinking about that time, I realized it was a jewel to hold on to. A long-lasting friendship came out of that night. In the days of bloody battle that had followed, the good times were like gold to soldiers.

I had found myself, without realizing it, lost within that night for a moment. Distant, fading trumpets weaning its beautiful chorus, as the cymbals tapped a light rumble. Gliding my lovely lady across the dance floor like a swan. All eyes gazed upon the glow of her white dress as it shined off the hard wood floor. Never had I seen a more gorgeous creature in all the world and not a more perfect moment than that one. After that night, Vasyl and I knew what was worth fighting for. It wasn't the money or pride. This woman had become the only reason left for coming back alive. I knew Vasyl and I had to make it through this mission to Japan.

"You can snap out of it anytime my friend!" Vasyl laughed, he knew how easily I was distracted.

We arrived at the station, hungry and unbearably tired. We slowed to begin our decent.

"Bay Front Station, come in Brazil! Fuel Port Twelve?" there was no answer, which was to be expected so I tried again.

"This is Crow! Permission to land and refuel as scheduled!"

Something was clearly not right.

"Seagull, what's going on?" I asked, believing maybe I needed to switch radio bands.

There was no response from Vasyl either. Things went wrong before I could even think about what move to make next.

I saw his plane not far in front of my own and still had no idea why he said nothing when I had called on the radio. Quickly, I saw him pull up his landing gear and swerve to the left. I shouted over the radio, "Seagull, what's going on?"

Out of nowhere, ground artillery shot off a couple rounds by Vasyl and then pounded the side of my jet. I yelled down at them, "Friendly! Friendly, this is Seagull! Why are you firing on us?"

No response came from Bay Front Station Twelve.

I maneuvered quickly and shocked myself at the plane's ability to function under fire. It was no use though against five separate anti-aircraft gunners. I swung left, then right, and looked over just in time to see Vasyl's right wing and engine being ripped clean off. He went down in a ball of flames.

"Vasyl!" I shouted over the radio, as if it would have reversed what I had just witnessed.

I hoped against all odds that he would be fine, as foolish as it sounded. My own survival took a back seat for a second as I saw the flames. The artillery sprayed the sky as I tried to evade it, knowing it was simply only a matter of time. One hit and then another took out my left engine. Shrapnel pierced through the cockpit, grazing my face and splintering my hands. This was the end for me, I thought.

Soon, I was gliding in on one engine close to the tree tops. The left engine, leaking fuel, finally caught on fire.

"God, if you can hear me," I prayed, thinking of Maria and how bad I had messed up taking on this mission.

In my mind, it was the end for sure, as the plane rattled to pieces. I tried to set her down softly, but that was almost impossible. As I looked at the tall jungle trees, I knew it was going to hurt. I thought about my best friend, painfully burning alive. One thump and then another crack reverberated through the cockpit as my jet fell below the canopy.

Two paths had been lit by the inferno of both planes. Vasyl crashed down some distance ahead of me, I was unsure of how far at the time. A loud crack broke past the strange calm that lasted a mere seconds, as my plane collided with one tree then another. The entire jet was launched into a spiral just before slamming into the landscape. I thank God I was barely conscious for that final impact into the dirt.

All was a blur. As I opened my eyes, I knew I'd been fortunate to end up with the cockpit on its side, rather than upside down. Unfortunate however, was that all that remained of a very expensive prototype was a mangled mess. My last thought was of the mission, which we had obviously failed. Had we been intercepted? Would our mission be known by the Americans? One thing was certain, I had to make it out of here and see Maria again.

I pulled on my harness straps. As they released, my face hit the shield of the cockpit, which had opened during the impact. Quickly, I grabbed the edge of the shield and pulled myself out onto the ground. My whole body ached. It quickly became apparent I had no broken bones, but plenty of cuts and bruises, even a near concussion.

I did not known then, but a plan at the Bay Front re-fueling sta-tion was well underway. Americans had discovered it. It was a tip off for sure. It wouldn't be until years later that I would dis-cover that those same Americans had also been manipulated and weren't even aware of it.

Shouts rang out from the station.

"Walters, take a squad with you and search the jungle. Make sure you get as much of those planes back here as you can."

"Yes, Sir"

"Corporal, if you find Fredric alive, kill him quick and bury the body deep!" "Understood, Captain. What about Vasyl, Sir?"

"If you locate him alive, bring that traitor to me and I'll per-sonally see to it that he burns".

The Corporal continued, "Attention! Everyone quiet down! It goes without saying but we need excellence, even perfection on this one."

The men all shouted in agreement.

"As you all know, our retrieval ship will be here in four hours. That's a small window to do what needs to be done. I believe in each one of you, even if most of you have only served under me for a short time."

"You heard the Captain! Short, sweet, we clean up, we leave!"

A second explosion from the fuel left over in one of my engines was all that was needed to help them find me. The ground rat-tled as I felt the heat from the flames only yards away, burning a portion of my torn pants as I laid on the ground. I felt sick and vomited on the hard dirt when I awakened to consciousness.

The only thing broken was my pride, though my face was considerably bruised up. I felt nothing right away, still in shock about everything that had just occurred in mere seconds.

What the hell just happened? We were told no issues, it would be a near straight shot. We should have gone over Russia instead of taking the long way around. I was certain nothing could have caught up to us in those jets! Second guessing the mission now was useless of course. It was time to start walking, to stay ahead of the men at the station and find Vasyl. Hopefully, somehow, he made it out alive and was already ahead of me.

The jungle was thick and even harder to see through with all the smoke from the fire that had begun to spread. The heat was even more unbearable. Sweat started beading down my forehead into my open wounds. As I struggled my way through the thick branches, I tore off a piece of my sleeve to cover my mouth and nose. The smoke covered the area like a blanket as I drew closer to where Vasyl had gone down.

It was then I heard a faint, distant call, almost like the sound of an animal. At this point, I wasn't sure what the source of this odd noise was. Risking my own safety, I yelled out in the direction I heard the sound, "Vasyl!"

Cries of agony came through the jungle, so I moved as fast as I could.

"Fredric," I was not prepared to see what was left of the man I'd known.

My shock at the sight of him was almost uncontainable, as I made my way over to his half charred body leaning against a tree trunk. All I could think of was how he could still be alive and how painful his last moments were going to be. I could not hold back my tears. Vasyl looked at me, half his face burned off.

I was completely unsure of what, if anything, could be done for him. In his panic, he had ejected before the jet blew up. However, the explosion had still caught up to him and torched up the side of his body and his chute. I said nothing except that I was sorry.

Vasyl turned his head slightly and gazed at me with his one good eye. This was a sight which would haunt my dreams for years.

"My name's not Vasyl," he said as his accent quickly faded.

My best friend had been lying to me all these years and yet he chose to speak the truth in his final moments. He laid there, grimacing through the pain and the shock of the events that had just transpired.

"We don't have much time, I'll tell you what I can. My name is Kevin Curtis. I have been undercover longer than you've known me".

My first thought was not that of betrayal. I was thinking what if he had died right away, would I ever have discovered this on my own? What he said next shattered my whole world as I knew it. I looked at him, and hearing what he said, it was as if the words were not real.

"Your wife was working with me. Her name is Samantha, not Maria. Before you stop me, just know that her love for you is, and always has been, real."

I wanted to convince myself that what he said was no more than a lie.

"She never wanted to hurt you and neither did I. You must understand, she planned an escape for us, but not quickly enough. Someone has changed it! I swear, this should not have happened at all."

"Samantha did not intend on falling in love with you. At first, you were just an assignment. Neither one of us thought for a second they would shoot you out of the sky."

His words said so much in such a short amount of time, changing everything. Even then, I knew what was most important, getting out of that jungle alive. For Kevin Curtis, it was far too late for that. I tried to prop him up so he would be able see ahead.

He grabbed my flight jacket by the collar and said, "Get yourself north. Live the life I will never have. Now, go!"

He placed in my hand a St. Christopher necklace his mother had given him as a boy. This was the last thing he did before I left his side. He had only hours left to live without medical treatment. The men behind us would reach Kevin well before then. As I walked away, I glanced back and saw him draw his gun, ready to fight to the end.

I wiped the sweat and small amount of blood that came from the wound above my eyebrow. However, no tears would come that day. My anger had forced them from me.

I whispered aloud, "I'm sorry my friend, May God forgive you and grant you peace."

I would never again know another friend like Kevin. This was when I noticed more of my own pain from the crash. Though not severe, it made the task of running that much more difficult.

Thirty minutes had passed. I push my way deeper into the jungle as it continued to burn behind me. I heard the sound of several gun shots before the echoes tapered off into silence. How did things manage to get worse when everything seemed perfect just hours ago? Everything I thought I knew had turned out to be a lie.

I was not with Kevin for his final stand, the way I had been countless times before. Even now, I struggle with guilt over it. I know he would have thought it best one of us live, than both of us die. It was that moment, fighting to survive, when I decided to live my life the way I imagined he would have wanted me to.

I knew as soon as those thoughts crossed my mind, evil men were descending upon Kevin. Their purpose, of which, I did not know.

THE HUNT

"**A**pproaching the site of the first plane fallen now."

The flames were almost extinguished.

"We won't be able to salvage much of this plane" another soldier said.

He glanced across the wreckage, and through the smoke, saw a figure leaning against a tree. It was Kevin. But what the soldier failed to notice, was Kevin's arm raised, pistol in hand. He fired suddenly, glaring at the men with his one good eye. A slight grin formed on his face as he yelled, "Who's ready?"

His first shot hit the young soldier in the center of his head.

"Shooter! Everyone get down!" yelled the commanding officer.

An eruption of gunfire permeated the jungle. Kevin continued to fire blindly at the men. The Americans, enraged by the sudden loss of their own, attempted to hit back. The chaos, in reality, lasted mere minutes, but seemed more like an eternity. Then as quickly as it started, all shots ceased on Kevin's end.

The men slowly closed in on the shooter, guns in their firing position. What they saw was a lifeless Kevin, pistol tightly gripped in his hand. Although it was a relief to find him dead, this was not the man they had hoped to find.

"There's a separate pair of footprints leading away from him, Sir," one of the soldiers observed.

"Fredric was here for sure," the Commander replied.

After assessing the scene for himself, the Commander continued, "Alright gentlemen, we have ourselves a man hunt. I want six of you with me and the rest of you will finish the clean-up here. Fredric knows he's out-numbered, but we know this jungle better than anyone. We will not return to camp empty handed. Men, head out!"

Meanwhile, heading north a mile into the jungle, I struggled with seemingly no escape. I was bleeding and in severe pain, only able to move at a moderate rate. Circumstances were getting increasingly worse, as the sun said good night, and darkness approached. I was becoming desperate, and did the only thing I could think of to do. I prayed.

"God, I know I was never much of a praying man. Honestly, I don't even believe you are there. But, I need your help, a miracle."

Despite my efforts, I knew I was already dead. I sat down at the base of a tree trunk to rest. I closed my eyes tightly and soon I was in a dreamland, away from the horrible nightmare I was currently in. Then I saw her face.

"Fredric!"

"Yes, Maria?"

"You'd better get moving, you'll miss your train," she said, while setting the table for breakfast.

This was a dream I wished was a reality.

The Commander and his men were closer than ever at this point to reaching Fredric. The heat and incessant pestering of the mosquitoes were the only things slowing them down. The sun was beginning to set, as the men took out their emergency lights.

"Shouldn't we set up camp, sir?" one of the soldiers asked.

"You know as well as I do, if we stop, we'll lose him!"

As the crew reluctantly continued on their path, a calm, almost frightening peace, seemed to lay upon the entire area.

"Nios guloin scoila."

"What the hell was that? Anyone else just hear that?" one of the men asked, his nerves on edge.

"Keep moving son! It was just an animal," the Commander said.

The voice came again, "Nios guloin scoila."

"There's someone else out here!" the same man yelled.

His fears were quickly swept under the rug once again, as the men pushed forward with their mission. Their machetes cut through the brush like a hot knife through butter, while the spotlights gleamed through the haze of the smoke left over.

Rain began to fall swiftly throughout the jungle, steaming as it hit the sun dried leaves. I awoke from my deep sleep, still leaning against the tree trunk. I knew they were not far behind me. I could hear the breaking of branches and saw the cascading light beams cut in and out of the trees. The heckling of their voices echoed through the valley.

"We know you're out here and we know you're wounded! Why don't you just make this easier on everyone and show yourself! I promise we will make it quick and painless!"

The pain was getting worse and their voices were getting closer.

"Come on Fredric, you must have known we couldn't just let you walk away," a man was suddenly standing before me.

Before I knew it, my head was slammed back into the tree trunk. I was momentarily rendered unconscious. Whispers began to run through the haze as I returned to the present. I felt myself being dragged, the dirt pulling at my clothes. I heard rushing water getting louder and louder. The moon began to break in and out of the canopy as I tried to come to grips with my surroundings.

"Please, don't do this," my voice breaks along with the searing pain in my head.

"Jason, deal with him! I don't want to hear him beg!"

"Sorry about this, but someone always has to pay," said the man, presumably Jason, as he shoves a rag in my mouth.

"I don't have time for this! I'll see you both back at camp. I don't have to remind you what will happen if you're late." another man said.

"Yes, Sir!" replied Jason and the other man in unison

The man addressed as 'Sir', proceeded to walk back on the path they created, leading to their camp.

"Carter, grab his legs, I got his arms."

"Careful who you're barking orders to, Jason. You forgetting your place?"

Everything was dark now and I didn't know if I was alive or dead. I could still hear the sound of rushing water next to me, so I must have been alive. The moon finally broke over a small cluster of trees and I was able to see an opening to a cave, just behind the waterfall I had been hearing.

The glistening water revealed that all my wounds had mysteriously vanished. Blood remained on my skin, but there was no source. How am I still alive? It was simply not possible. I felt no more pain, only a sense of confusion. I was alone. Jason and Carter had let me live, and now, they were nowhere in sight.

Seeking shelter from the night, I was drawn into the cave. With uncertainty, I grasped both sides of the wall, feeling my way deeper into the cave. I was blind in the pitch black, but to me, it was obvious this was a tunnel, not just a cave. I had no weapons and no food. They had left me with only the clothes on my back. I had no way of getting back to my Samantha.

I heard a sound vibrate through the tunnel, pulling me out of my self-pity. The ground I was standing on began to shake. This 'earthquake' revealed a light gleaming through one of the rocks. I ran over to the light source and began pulling at the rocks and trying to lift the boulders, until all the strength I had left was gone.

Out of nowhere, the light slowly faded before I could see where it originated from. I quickly began to crawl through the hole I had just created in the rocks. It was almost too small to get through without some crafty maneuvering.

On the other side of the passage, I could see an opening in the center of the roof. The light of the full moon beamed upon the roots grown into the ruins from the jungle floor. In this room on the far wall, lay a set of three identical spears. Each one displayed an intricate design. What had I just discovered? What was this place?

As I sifted through the rubble left behind from the cave-in of the ceiling, I found what looked to be a torch wrapped in a cloth. It seemed to be already partially used. I rummaged through my pockets to find my metal case containing matches. It was no surprise they were all wet, except one. I held my breath as I struck the match against the rocks. Thankfully, the match lit and I set fire to the torch.

What the light revealed that day, I will never forget. It was forever seared into my brain. The remains of what looked like a Roman soldier laid before me. His bones were in full gear, with a battle sword still in hand. As I moved closer to the skeleton, I could see a necklace hanging next to it. It held a small disc with some sort of symbol in the center. I could not take my eyes off this necklace.

"Why am I so drawn to this?" I asked myself aloud.

Just before my hands could grasp it, a white glow, like the one that had led me to the room, started to emanate from the symbol. With no fear or explanation, I clutched the necklace and put it over my head. It rested on my chest as I continued to gaze at it. All normal reasoning vanished and curiosity took over. I should have just climbed through the ceiling and got the hell out of there, but this necklace continued to entrance me, as the light enveloped the entire chamber.

Two hours later back at the refueling station, the men started to load pieces of the disassembled jet air crafts on to their ship.

"Men, I want those pieces completely secure before we board. Then we can go home heroes!" the Commander ordered.

"Yes, Sir!" exclaimed the men with excitement.

"Have we taken care of our little situation in the jungle, Carter?" the Commander continued.

"Both pilots are dead, sir. I saw to Fredric myself," Carter lied through his teeth.

No sooner were those words from his mouth uttered when a flash of bright light appeared from the south, only for a split second.

"What the hell was that?" said one of the men.

"I'm not sure, but we are not wasting any time to find out. We're leaving now!" the Commander shouted.

The light planted questions in the heart of every man out there that day. Some were very afraid and stepped up the pace in securing all their gear on the ship.

"What happened? Where am I? Anybody here?" I screamed, staring up at the white ceiling.

"Fredric, stop yelling, you'll scare the patients."

"Samantha? Is that you?"

"I still can't get over you calling me by my real name. After all those years pretending to be Maria. I hope you're still not upset with me."

"How did I get here? The last thing I remember was the light," complete and utter confusion overcame me.

"Honey, don't be silly. You were just telling me all about your ordeal in Brazil. You're still at St. Mary's in New Mexico. We found you almost dead on the border, lying flat on your back, mumbling to yourself."

I was still stunned, "Samantha is that really you? I thought I would never see you again."

"I love you too Fredric. You're too funny, I've been here all week. I wouldn't leave you for the world. It wasn't easy for me to get back over here. After four years of being undercover, they destroyed my file in case something went wrong. Anyways, enough of that, you need your rest. When you're better, we are going to start a new life together. I'm thinking about somewhere in Pennsylvania."

I had always dreamed of a quiet life on the east coast of America. Pennsylvania seemed like a great place to do just that. I couldn't believe my wife was standing in front of me, it seemed too good to be true.

How did I end up on the U.S. Border? As hard as I tried, all I could remember was that symbol on the necklace.

Samantha interrupted my thoughts, "Rest up, Fredric. The doctor says you will be able to leave the day after tomorrow."

On her way out the door, she stopped to ask me something I found peculiar, "You never mentioned where you got that necklace. Was that in Morocco?"

Much to my surprise, the necklace was still with me. I didn't remember, but I must have put it on. Before I could ponder the thought any longer, my eyes became heavy. As I slowly dosed off, I muttered to Samantha, "You know, you still have some making up to do for that whole mess back home."

"Yes Fredric, I know," she giggled.

A New Dawn

"**M**orning, Eric. I thought you said you were going to wake me up."

"Sorry, dear. I forgot, in too much of a hurry. I have so much to do at the office. I made a fresh pot of coffee for you and breakfast for the kids is sitting on the table."

The gleam in Sara's eyes was more from shock than anything else. Very rarely did I make breakfast for myself, let alone the rest of the family.

"What's the special occasion for this surprise breakfast?" she asked as she made her way to the bathroom, to begin her two hour ritual we call 'getting ready for the day'.

"Nothing, I just happened to wake up a little earlier than usual," I replied.

"You had another one of your dreams again, didn't you?" Sara continued.

ETERNAL

"Yeah," I mumbled.

"You should really see someone about that," she said with concern, while stepping into the shower.

Shuffling through my stuff in the dresser drawer, I frantically looked for my watch. I knew I had set it down around here last night.

"Have you seen my watch, hun?"

"Nope. You mean the one Fredric gave you?" Sara hollered from the shower.

"Yes, of course that one. You know I always wear Dad's watch and suit to important meetings," I said.

"I think it's on the shelf above the bed. Can you come here for a second?"

What now? Sometimes I wondered if Sara even understood the meaning of 'being in a hurry'. It never seemed to be important unless she had to be somewhere on time. As much as I loved her, she could still be extremely frustrating sometimes.

I quickly downed another cup of coffee and slurped up the remains of cereal in my bowl, as I rushed to meet Sara's request.

"Yes, dear?"

"Don't forget to drop the twins off at school," she said.

"You know I don't have time for that," I responded, slight irritation came through my voice.

Sara stepped out of the shower and began to dry off her hair. She shot me that very common look of sternness, trying to get her message across.

"Eric, I have a very busy day too. It's finals this week. I told you yesterday. You never seem to listen to me."

37

"I'm sorry," I hugged her with assurance to prevent another argument I would surely lose.

"Don't worry, I'll take the boys to school. Then, I will see you at Mom's tonight after work?" I continued.

"Yes, I will meet you there. Thank you Eric." Sara said, relief in her eyes.

The prospective clients I would be meeting with soon had made Sara and I reservations at some fancy joint downtown, Mom had offered to watch the boys. Apparently, these people were extremely confident I would accept their offer and Sara was not one to turn down an all-expenses paid date night.

I gave her a quick kiss, then went to retrieve the boys. I found them in the kitchen, still working on their breakfast I had prepared for them.

"Okay boys, you have ten minutes to finish up. We don't need to be late again. Daddy has a big day ahead of him."

"We want to play in the leaves," David and Michael pleaded in unison.

"When you get home after school," I really didn't have time to argue with the twins.

After corralling the boys into the car, we were finally on the road, headed to the school. I couldn't help but think of how fast they were growing up. It seemed like just yesterday I was holding them in my arms at the hospital, while Dad proceed to give me advice on how to raise them. Now, they were in kindergarten.

We pulled up to the elementary school, the kids were less than enthused. They hopped out of the car and waved back at me on their way up to the double doors. Now, it was time for Daddy's day to start, I thought to myself.

On the way to the office, I remembered that tomorrow was Veteran's Day. Dad deserved a gift, I would pick him up something before I saw him tonight.

As I approached downtown Philadelphia, all I could think about was the dream I kept having. What did it all mean? Who was the woman, dying in my arms? Why did I have to take her to the light? It had been nearly three weeks of having this reoccurring dream and I still didn't understand it. Maybe Sara was right, I should probably talk to someone about it.

An elevator ride, up twenty-three floors, brought me to the top of the Marion Building, where Cove Corporation was located. Many years of hard work and sacrifices had created one of the largest privately contracted excavating companies. Today, we would land our greatest contract to date.

The elevator opened to the main office. Nervousness collided with excitement, I knew this was the day we would really put our name on the map.

Our lovely receptionist greeted me with a smile, "Mr. Richards, the prospective clients are waiting for you in the conference room."

"Thank you, Lisa," I smiled back.

I took one more deep breath before entering the conference room. This was it.

"Gentlemen, thank you for coming. Let's get right down to business. There must be great interest in this dig, judging by your level of government authority. I'd be lying if I said I wasn't a little bit surprised. We, at Cove Corporation, have handled some of the most historically important dig sites in the world, ever since my father started this company."

Before I could continue, one of the men interrupted me, "Mr. Richards, I represent a special group of individuals, which will remain nameless. I can guarantee you, we have the best interest of this country at heart. Each of these gentlemen sitting before you are some of the best geologists and physicists in their respective fields. So, I speak for everyone here, when I say skip the sales pitch."

"Excuse me?" I said in disbelief.

"We chose you and your company because we already know you are the best in the world at what you do. Our question to you, Mr. Richards, is can you deliver without any questions?"

The look of every man in the room seemed to pierce right through me. I had no time to ponder the unusual question.

"Yes, of course," I managed.

"And your crew also, can they guarantee us complete secrecy?"

"Yes, sir," things were becoming more odd.

The sternness upon the man's face said it all. Any words spoken between us today were to remain in this room, and the names of anyone involved were to remain anonymous. If something were to go awry, these were the type of men to ensure that my body would never be found. Could I keep a secret this big? For the amount of money that was surely involved, I would take this to my grave.

"Good. Now Mr. Richards, you will be told the location of the site on the specified day, no sooner," said the man, while unrolling a map.

There was an unusual gleam in the eyes of the other four men at the table, as the man began to speak figures while pointing at the map.

"Now, most of us have heard the stories and seen the footage of the sunken ship off the coast of Brazil. Everyone knows it was a large military force of some kind. But we believe it to be American, on a top secret mission in 1944, to retrieve two prototype jet aircraft. The aircraft have been identified as German. However, we do not know why the ship's crew fell ill and ultimately never made it back to the United States. According to the Captain's journal, the men quickly became sick after leaving the re-fueling station."

"His final entry states: 'We have become deathly ill now, only a couple hours after leaving shore. This seems to be an unnatural sickness. The five remaining members of the crew and myself, believe it was the flash of light that made us sick. Perhaps it was radioactive or maybe it was something emanating from a temple we found. I do believe this to be true. My lieutenant believes our water supply was poisoned. The rest of us left alive, will do what we can to keep the air crafts from falling into the wrong hands. I fear our fate has already been sealed. God, please forgive us for what we have done. Grant us peace in heaven.'"

"This 'temple' that the captain so subtly mentions, is what we are after. The reason we are waiting to begin is a simple one."

Curiosity gripped my heart. Why the sudden interest in this story now, after all these years? Why were they willing to spend so much money to search for a temple that may or may not exist? My questions were many and I knew these were not the type of men to hand out answers like presents on Christmas.

"We will start searching as soon as we have pin-pointed the exact location. We will start with the excavation of the ship, as that may lead to more clues on the whereabouts of the temple. We believe the ship may be washed up inland, within a two square mile radius."

The man looked around the room, as if awaiting approval, then concluded, "That will be all for now."

Stepping out of the conference room, I was handed the initial contract. The number of zeros on the proposed pay out quickly dispersed whatever concerns I had. I was on a need to know basis. Honestly, at that moment, I didn't care about knowing anything. I could retire on that amount of money. Although I did love this place, being egotistical, I knew it would fall apart without me. I chuckled to myself. Maybe I would just give everything to Sara and the kids.

For now, I had only one thing to think about, Dad's present. I hoped he was feeling better today.

The men waited until Eric left the room to talk amongst themselves.

"Carter, do we have control of this situation? You know damn well the boss would not be very pleased if we screw this up again."

"I have it handled, Jason. We're going to meet with Eric's father and this time, he will have nowhere to run."

"What makes you think he will cooperate this time?"

"I'm going to search Fredric's mind. He will gladly show us where that amulet is."

The drive to the mental hospital was long, as usual. I couldn't help but think about what had just transpired in the conference room. Something was off about those men, something I couldn't quite put my finger on. But now was not the time to figure that out. Now it was time to visit with Dad. The leaves rustled as I entered the hillside parking lot at Lakeview Center. On an overcast day like today, this was one of the eeriest places. The hospital's grounds were always perfectly manicured and it looked like someone had cut the grass by hand with scissors.

Dad had called this place home for that past two years. Our family was still not sure what had happened to him on that summer day. He was found on the side of the street, laying on the concrete sidewalk, mumbling to himself, just three blocks from the house. According to Mom, he had a similar episode decades before sometime during the war.

I knew this place well and proceeded into the main entrance, down the well-lit hallway, and through the magnetic locking doors. I slipped past the waiting room, bypassing security and checked in at the desk. Everyone knew me by name.

The doctor met me at the desk, "Good evening, Mr. Richards. If you would follow me, we had to move your father to E Wing about four days ago."

We had to stop and wait every few minutes for the locks to turn green.

When we reached Dad, I stopped the Doctor just outside his room, "Why did you move him?"

"During routine snack and recreation time, your father lost control. He became extremely violent and started throwing chairs at the other patients. He kept yelling and repeating, 'the evil is inside of them'. We feared for his safety as well as our other patients. But no need to worry, Mr. Richards, we have been taking good care of him. But, you will need to make your visit short today, it's almost time for his dinner and medication. I will be just outside if you need me."

The doctor seemed genuinely concerned. But honestly, why would I not worry? My dad tried to wound, and even kill his fellow patients! Why didn't Mom tell me?

I looked into the room. There, on the floor, in the corner of the room, sat the shell of a man. He was curled up, his knees to his chest, rocking back and forth. I couldn't believe this man was my father. Fredric Richards, the war hero I had heard so much about, was now broken.

"They're coming for me, I can feel it. The evil ones, they want the light. You can't let the evil inside. Protect the light. They're everywhere!"

"Dad, it's me, Eric."

"Go away. Get away from me, son. It's not good for you. Oh, my head! They're still inside!"

"Dad, stop! There's no one here, just me. I brought you a gift. It's a model of a plane, like the ones you use to fly. You remember flying, don't you?"

He grasped the small model plane, and for a moment, it seemed like something inside him changed. His eyes widened as he stared intently at it. A single tear streamed slowly down his gray beard.

He finally spoke coherently, "Oh, yes! What fun we had, me and Kevin. Poor Kevin. He was the real hero, so brave, a foolish friend 'til the very end."

It wasn't long before his mind was overtaken again and he began to mumble, "Go. We have to go. What a beautiful light."

"I'm sorry, Dad. I have to go. I love you," I couldn't take it anymore.

I walked out of the room, trying to suppress the lump forming in my throat. I passed an orderly at the door, delivering my father's dinner and medication.

It was twenty minutes later by the time I had gotten past all the magnetic locking doors. I opened the door to my Jeep and collapsed into the seat, mentally exhausted in such a short time.

I flipped the switch to the radio to drown out any discouraging thoughts of my father. An announcer came through, relaying today's world events, "President Reagan is scheduled to meet with diplomatic leaders in Russia today to discuss current relational issues on both sides..."

I quickly turned it off. The news was just as depressing as Lakeview. Despite the situation with Dad, today was a good day. I couldn't complain too much, after I had just landed such a massive contract at work. Keeping that thought firmly in the front of my mind, I proceed to Mom's house, where I would meet Sara and the kids. I couldn't wait to tell Sara the good news.

LOSS OF A SOLDIER

I was only a few minutes late, but I knew Mom would call me out on it as soon as I walked in the door.

Sure enough, she did, "You're late!"

Sara came to my rescue, chiming in from the kitchen, "Mom, would you let him in already? Stop bantering him, it's cold outside."

"Relax, you two. We can only stay for a little bit, our reservations are for eight."

I didn't like going over to Mom's after Dad had gone off the deep end. I could see how upset she still was, despite her best efforts to deny it. It made me sad when I thought of him curled up in the corner, lost within his tortured mind.

Mom had what you would call a modest house. She always seemed to have a special touch in making it feel like home. It also helped that she was a fantastic cook. The cooking, I believe, is what kept Dad close to home, before the breakdown. She had a rustic, turn of the century home, common to the Philadelphia area. Brick walls enclosed the three bedrooms, two baths, and decent-sized attic. The attic was always in shambles. It contained all of Dad's belongings and Mom refused to go up there. There were too many memories.

"Thank you Mom for watching the twins," I said.

"You're welcome son. Hope you're not expecting me to do this all the time," she said jokingly, Mom loved spending time with the boys.

She continued, "They're up in your old room playing with that video game thing you bought. I don't really like them spending too much time on those things, but it does seem to keep them occupied. I especially don't like that you spent so much money on it."

"It's alright Mom, we can afford it now," I said with a sense of pride.

With the payout I would be getting on this new project, we could afford a lot of video games, I thought to myself. I kissed David and Michael good night and gave Mom a big hug. Then I escorted Sara out to the Jeep and we made our way to the restaurant.

"Here we are," I said enthusiastically.

"Are you sure this is the place, Eric?" Sara had a puzzled look on her face. "It sure is."

Just the entrance alone had a plush, red carpet and golden railings. A slate staircase led to a glass, rotating door, the trim being gold as well. The front was equipped with four of these doors to accommodate the high volume of customers. From floor to ceiling, the place screamed of elegance, refinement, and exclusiveness. It was so high class that every pair of eyes that landed on us, gave us the feeling we didn't belong.

"My word Eric! Would you look at that?" Sara said, her eyes wide, gazing in the direction of the waterfall.

Centered in the dining area, there was a beautiful marble and granite waterfall display. Its tall columns stretched nearly twenty-two feet. From there, the water showered down to the circular base, covered with colored lights.

"Yes, it is quite nice," I knew it would be a wonderful dinner tonight.

"It was so nice of those gentlemen to reserve a table for us here tonight," she commented, as the hostess found our name on her clipboard and showed us to our seats.

Yes, they definitely had some deep pockets and strong connections I could only dream of. Something still seemed a bit odd to me, I thought, thinking of the suit that had been placed in my office and the dress delivered to Sara.

"What's wrong hun?" Sara asked.

"I was just wondering why that man was so insistent on paying for this extravagant dinner tonight."

"Eric, you worry too much. Besides, when was the last time we had a night out without the boys?"

"You're right, it's been too long, and I must say, you look amazing in that white dress," although all I could think about was taking it off.

She knew exactly what I was thinking and before she could shoot me the evil eye, the waiter arrived at our table to take our order. Sara proceeded to relay her order. As she did, time seemed to slow down, as I gazed at her intently. I remembered the first time we met back in college. I was chasing my dreams and Sara was already living hers. She considered it a simple joy to be able to attend college. Her family was all too familiar with living in poverty, after her mom died when she was young. Sara assumed the role of raising her younger brother, while they lived off their father's custodial wages.

The waiter interrupted my reminiscing. I quickly gave him my order, then started scanning the large dining area again. We were suddenly in the land of the wealthy and for a moment, we felt like we belonged. Everyone was dressed to impress. Some were adorned with extravagant jewelry, while others wore authentic furs and sophisticated hats. After this contract I had accepted, we could be like this if we wanted.

I decided now was the time to share the good news with Sara, but before I could, a man stood up and gathered everyone's attention.

"Welcome everyone to the Grand Hotel. My name is Alex Reuben and this is my establishment. I do hope you enjoy your meal tonight. I can vouch for the chefs and I assure you, you will. Although there was that incident where I became violently ill," he said, looking over at the head chef, both laughing.

"Of course, I failed to inform them of my intolerance to peanuts!" Mr. Reuben added.

The room erupted with soft laughter.

"I have handpicked each and every one of you here tonight. We have scientists, geologists, linguistics, doctors, and ex-military specialists joining us this evening. Please hit the lights and bring up the slide map of Brazil."

Mr. Reuben took out a laser pointer and continued with his presentation, "We know that somewhere on the southern coast of Brazil, there is the most amazing geological, not to mention historical, find of ancient Mayan culture. A very similar culture inhabited this area. Preliminary carbon dating from artifacts uncovered last year, puts this civilization there long before the Mayans. We are still uncertain and must reveal the truth."

"In this unconfirmed civilization, we also believe there to be a rather large burial of gold. Myself, as well as my colleagues, feel that we are just days away from knowing the exact location of the site. We are looking for a temple that has been overtaken by the jungle. Please be alert and prepared, as we could be shipping out in a matter of weeks."

Then, Alex Reuben proceeded to clap his hands, signaling the waiters to bring out the food.

"Good night, and enjoy your evening!" he concluded.

A beautiful woman arrived next to him, linking her arm in his, followed by his security detail.

Sara was in awe of what she had just heard from this strange man. I knew she must have been slightly irritated, not hearing such big news from me first. But she just looked at me, pure love in her eyes, like she was the proudest woman on earth of her husband.

The elegant evening with Sara had come to a close and we were on our way back to Mom's house.

"How was your dad today?" she asked.

I didn't want to think about my emotional visit with my father, but instead wanted to revel in the wonderful night I just had with my wife.

"It was just more out of routine than anything else," I replied, smiling and deflecting the reality of my father's condition.

"He seems to be about the same. Except, when I gave him that model plane, it must have brought back bad memories," that was being subtle.

Little did I know, about forty miles away, an evil was on the rise. This sinister disturbance, so innocently disguised, would change our lives forever.

Back at Lakeview Center, a very tired Fredric Richards was prepared to be wheeled back to his room. The orderlies assigned to Fredric made one stop at the nurse's station for his new medication.

"Patient Fredric Richards here for his medication."

It was here at the medication office, where all hell broke loose. It was an event that would baffle the authorities for years to come.

The man behind the window glanced at Fredric, then stared intently at the two orderlies.

"I don't recognize you gentlemen." the nurse said.

Carter was caught off guard and quickly responded, "We're new to the staff, making our first rounds tonight."

Believing that would stifle any further inquiries from the nurse, Jason reached for the meds. A doctor arrived next to the nurse and snatched Jason's wrist.

"I'm in charge of this facility, gentlemen. I personally hired everyone on staff here," said the doctor.

With this, Jason became furious, his eyes began to darken.

"You shouldn't have done that doctor," Carter said, recognizing Jason's angry face.

In an instant, almost too fast for the human eye to witness, Jason snapped the doctor's hand like a twig. Part anger and part evil glee showed through in his maniacal smile. His veins began to darken in the manner his eyes did, moving down his arms. A powerful force escaped through his fingertips, which launched the doctor through the adjacent window, making him land on the pavement outside.

"Jason, cool it!" Carter yells, "Was that really necessary?"

"No, but is sure was fun," Jason said smiling, his arm still in the air, while the broken window let in the storm from outside.

"Jason, I'm doing this right here, right now, while we still have time. We can't fail Alex again."

Carter looked over at Jason, as if there were a genuine understanding of what had to be done next.

"Alright, make it quick. I'll be outside standing watch," Jason said, leaving Carter with Fredric.

Carter placed both hands on either side of Fredric's head, as he sat in his wheelchair. Fredric was helpless as Carter's eyes and hands began to grow darker, as Jason's had. He stared straight through Fredric, almost as if to see the old man's soul.

"It's been a long time Fredric, did you miss us? This time, there won't be any interruptions. You're going to show me where it is and then we will find the source."

Fredric's body began to hover in the air above his wheelchair.

"You will remember! Show me!"

As Carter continued to shout, his power systematically increased. His eyes and arms still black as night, as what looked to be a shot, streamed forth hitting Fredric. In an instant, Fredric's mind began to open up to Carter.

"I know you, both of you! You threw me into the waterfall! Then somehow..."

"That's right, Freddie. We tracked you down and left you for dead in Mexico. But you just wouldn't die!"

With this, Fredric began to shout even louder, "Evil! You're both evil!"

Carter punched the old man in the mouth to suppress his cries.

"Yes, and unlike you, we will never die."

Carter collected himself and then continued, "Let's go back, shall we? Back to '83...'80...'75...'70...yes, here we are. No amulet, but even better, didn't know you had kept a journal. That makes you the biggest fool, you left it in your house."

Carter had found what he needed and rested Fredric back in his wheelchair. The old man was riddled with searing pain.

"Did you think we wouldn't find out you took it?"

Fredric's nose and ears were bleeding. Through the immense pain in his head, he summoned the strength to say only a few more words.

"My boy's no idiot, he'll find out what you are. See if he helps you then."

Carter was standing in the doorway and became even angrier with every word spoken by Fredric. The force built up and escaped through his hands once again, striking Fredric in the head.

"Forgive me Samantha. I should have..." Fredric mumbled.

With that, Fredric Richards reached the end of his life and his fight.

A Date with Destiny

The funeral was less than a week later. It was the middle of November on a cold, but sunny day. It was far too quiet, almost as if the entire city of Philadelphia had come to a standstill to pay its respects to Fredric Richards. Sadly, it would be quite some time before anyone would discover the sacrifices this man had made for the greater good of us all.

Amidst the excruciating pain and sorrow, many questions still lingered in the air. It was no coincidence that on the same day my father died, my mother's house was robbed. It was a miracle Mom wasn't home when the burglars ransacked her home.

Tears streamed down Mom's face as she asked, "Do you think those thieves were responsible for Fredric's death? What could they have possibly wanted?"

I looked straight at the casket as it was lowered down. Amongst the dirt and snowflakes, it reached its final resting place.

"I promise Mother, I'll find out who did this and when I do..."

She quickly reacted to this and grabbed my arm, "Vengeance, son, belongs to God. You killing someone makes you no better than whoever did this to your father."

The peaceful service came to an end with the usual parting sermon. People began to file out of the cemetery as a young woman walked over to my family.

"Hello Mrs. Richards. My name is Agent Carla Munoz and I'm the special investigator for the FBI in charge of your husband's case. Can I ask you a few questions?"

Trying my best not to be too impolite, I stepped between the investigator and my mother, making my disapproval evident.

"Can't this wait, Ms. Munoz? His body isn't even cold yet! You people really do have the worst timing!"

Carla took a step back, acknowledging my irritation.

I continued, "If you have any questions, you can call my office. I'm her son, Eric Richards, and if you don't mind, I think it would be best if you respected the privacy of my family."

I honestly think I startled her with my unexpected response to her insensitivity. However, she took it quite well, revealing a much thicker skin than appearances would lead you to believe.

Without missing a beat, she replied, "Just trying to help, Sir. We'll talk tomorrow in private, Mr. Richards."

I held my mom as she wept into my chest. Sara stood by my side, clasping David and Michael's hands. I couldn't help feeling, as I'm sure many of us did, that an hour tribute to such a great man wasn't enough. My father's life, or anyone's life, could not be summed up in a mere moments.

The snow was falling heavily now. I watched my breath in the Philadelphia air as tried to come to terms with what had happened. I had to know why my father was killed. It was an urge, or rather a desire, for retribution and justice. This need had stolen my sleep, which had not come since that awful night.

The five of us systematically filed into the limo. We sat in silence while the driver pulled away from the cemetery. I looked at Mom, I could tell she hadn't slept in days either without the aid of pills.

"Where to, Ma'am?" the driver asked.

"Home, please." Mom answered.

I didn't want to say anything, but I had to, "You can't go home, Mom. Everything is still a mess and it's the scene of an investigation."

Without hesitation, she stopped me, "I don't care. I want to go home. That mess needs to be cleaned up. Fredric would never tolerate such a thing. I'm going home Eric, don't argue with me."

"Alright, home it is. But you need some rest first."

She reluctantly agreed as we pulled up to the house. I volunteered to start cleaning up so Mom could finally sleep. She walked straight to her bedroom as Sara put the boys to sleep in my old room. I stared at the tossed house, wondering where to start. As far as we could tell, nothing had been stolen. What on earth did they want? Was it really worth Dad's life?

Not a single item in the house remained untouched by their destructive hands. Pictures were smashed, windows broken, and furniture splintered. It looked as though a bomb had detonated in the living room. Trying to hold back tears that were returning, I reached for the broom.

Earlier in the same house, Carter and Jason arrived after killing Fredric.

"Let's do this!" Carter shouted as he exited the car, walking up the path to the house where Jason was already waiting.

Jason smiled with glee at the opportunity for some fun and mayhem. He laughed as he used his strength to send the front door off its hinges.

"Honey, I'm home!" he yelled, laughing some more.

"Alright, we're here to find the journal. No more messing around," said Carter.

He raised one hand, then the other, and everything in the room began to hover. His hands were steady as all the objects formed a group in the middle of the room.

"Jason, it's not here. Check upstairs and in the attic. I'll search the basement. I know it's here somewhere."

Carter performed the same routine with the basement, while Jason covered the second floor.

"Carter! In the attic, I found it!"

Carter rushed to the attic and looked through the doorway to find Jason crouched down, starring at a locked suitcase.

"It's in here, under some books!" exclaimed Jason with extreme excitement, a mission quickly accomplished.

Carter raised one hand towards the lock on the suitcase. With a single jolt of his wrist, the lock shattered and the suitcase flung open.

"Check it." ordered Carter.

"What, you don't trust my judgment? After all these decades together?" said Jason in disgust.

Carter stared at him intently, "Remember, you were the one that let Fredric walk after you couldn't pull the memories from him last time. Anyways, we don't have time for an argument. Alex said to get the information as fast as we can, by any means necessary. Now check the case!" "Relax Carter, its right here. It looks like Fredric wrote down his scattered memories.

They cover events from Germany to Brazil and the crash, before he lost his mind."

Jason continued scanning the journal, "Ah, here it is. It's about ten pages or so describing the place and waterfall, near some kind of cavernous entrance."

"Okay, tear out the pages and let's get the hell out of here. Fredric's wife could be home any minute and that would ruin everything," said Carter.

Jason did as he was told. Then, he stood up and raised both hands in front of him toward the floor, in an instant, both men vanished. The room was left behind in a mark of chaos, one that would never be forgotten.

Still starring at the shattered pieces of a broken chair, I wondered where to start. Flakes of debris fell to the floor like ashes. I couldn't help but see the pieces like that of my shattered family, by the events that had taken place. I must be strong for Sara, the kids, and Mom. There was still a job to do and I needed to focus on the upcoming task. I had received the call that night informing me I was scheduled to leave for Brazil. Not the best timing, but life must go on.

Morning came too quickly. I had only gotten a few hours of sleep and hoped to get a few more on the plane ride.

I crawled out of bed, doing my best not to wake Sara.

"Honey, where are you going?" she asked through half closed eyes.

"Don't worry Sara, I'll be back in a few days. Take care of the boys and look after Mom. The taxi is probably waiting outside, I have to go. I love you."

"I love you too, Eric. Be careful."

Leaning over, I kissed my wife on the forehead, the same way I had done countless times before. I quickly jumped in the shower, realizing I still had to stop by our house to pick up a few things. The hot water beaded down my face as I thought about the dream I had last night. It was the same one from weeks ago. It was mainly flashes of strange images, but that voice seemed so real. What did it mean? Maybe it meant nothing at all. Every time the dream returned, I was always in awe at how vivid it was, like I was actually there.

I wasn't sure how long we had been cleaning last night. It was long enough to leave all of us exhausted. Sara didn't even flinch as I crept past her, reaching for my jacket and watch. I had no time for breakfast. The taxi outside was honking its horn incessantly. I grabbed a bagel, treading through some of the rubble in the kitchen, and finally made it out the front door.

The driver was not happy when I requested to be taken to my house first. I'm sure Alex Reuben was paying him enough, the least he could do was give me an extra ten minutes. It didn't take me long before I had a small bag packed. I picked up the necklace Dad had left me and put it around my neck. I wasn't superstitious, but felt I had to wear it for good luck. Soon enough, I was out the door once again, en route to the airport. No turning back now.

My crew had been issued special passes, letting us skip security, taking us directly to the plane. It was a large military aircraft. When I arrived, nearly the entire crew was already there. They were scattered about on the tarmac, shouting at each other, while loading equipment onto the plane. A small private jet was parked next to it, being prepped for takeoff.

Airport staff were busy de-icing and going through pre-flight regulations. The excavation team was combing over maps, discussing different routes through the jungle. I scanned all the equipment that was strategically loaded into the aircraft.

"I see we're bringing Big Boy," this was the name I had given our over-sized tree cutter.

"Yes, Sir. Everything just as you requested," said one of the crew members.

Robert, my chief foreman and good friend, approached me and spoke softly out of respect for my current situation. It was odd, since he was more accustomed to shouting orders.

"Eric, how are you and the family holding up?"

"As best as we can," I told him.

"Are you sure you want to do this? You know I can handle them," Robert said, looking at the crew and placing his hand on my shoulder reassuringly.

"Thanks, but I'll be fine. We need this money, who knows how long it will be before another contract like this comes along," I said, forcing a smile.

With this, Robert turned towards the men scanning the maps. There must have been at least thirty men involved in this project. If anyone could corral that many people, it was Robert.

He lifted his hands in the air and shouted as loud as his God-given voice would go, "How long until everything is secured for travel?"

A voice shouted in return from inside the plane, "Five minutes, Sir!"

Without any warning, two military vehicles and a limo pulled up next to us. Ten men armed for battle stepped out of the hummers. Robert and I glanced at each other, a puzzled look on both our faces.

"I didn't invite them," I whispered.

Next, the driver of the limo stepped out and opened the back door for his passenger. This passenger was one, Alex Reuben. I should have known.

"No need to be afraid, gentlemen," he said with both excitement and confidence.

He continued, "Can I have everyone's attention? These men will be accompanying us to Brazil. It's simple protection for us all, should we encounter anyone with questionable motives."

Questionable motives? How strange.

Alex and his two bodyguards approached me, "Eric, I don't think you have had the pleasure of meeting my two best men. Carter, Jason, this is Eric Richards, the man heading up this project."

Both men shook my hand.

"I trust these men with my life. I want you to know that they are also at your disposal if you need them for anything," said Alex.

"Yes, Sir, thank you," although I couldn't help but think of all the men with heavy guns behind him.

I could sense the discomfort in every one of my crew members. I knew they could see the displeasure on my face as well. We had never needed this much muscle before. Why now?

I spoke with the utmost respect to Alex, "Sir, is it really necessary to have all these men accommodate us? My crew is going to be quite unnerved working around such heavy fire power."

Alex's face became stern. His manner was almost aggressive, a side of him far removed from the one I had seen at dinner.

Forcefully, with one finger in my face, he shouted, "Look, Mr. Richards, you signed a contract! No questions, remember? I already told you, this is for your safety!"

I was stunned, but he was not finished, "I'm paying for this, Mr. Richards. You order your men how you want, but in the end, I'm the one in charge!"

Then he walked closer to me, until his face was directly in front of mine, and quietly said, "Don't ever question me in front of my own men again."

Alex took one step back and clapped his hands to motion to everyone present, "Let's get this show on the road!"

"Yes, Sir!" everyone agreed.

The crew quickly finished loading the final pieces of equipment. Alex pointed and waved his hands, directing the men on where to put some of the instruments. The crew began boarding the plane, Robert and I followed.

Alex stopped us before we could step in the plane, "Eric, Robert, you two are riding with me in the jet."

What a turnaround. I had just learned not to argue with this man, so Robert and I did as we were told and walked up the steps into the jet.

"Next stop, Brazil!" Alex said excitedly.

Robert and I sat in silence, not sure how to react to this gesture, as the jet left the runway.

Shortly after takeoff, Alex broke the tension and motioned to the stewardess, "My friends and I would like a drink."

So now we were friends? This guy couldn't seem to make up his mind. I was hoping for the best, as far as this dig was concerned, but I knew he would fight me during the whole process.

The woman was very beautiful and soft spoken as she asked me, "Would you like anything, Sir?"

I wasn't much of a drinker, but didn't want to create any more waves, so I replied, "I'll have your best stout, thank you."

Robert, on the other hand, was known for his love of all things alcohol. Without missing a beat, he requested a glass of scotch. I had nearly fired him on our last job because of this. He had caused a cave in while operating the bulldozer while he was intoxicated. Luckily, no one was hurt. Lucky for Robert, he was a longtime friend of mine, an aspect that had spared his job. My favoritism had unearthed some irritation amongst some of the other men.

Once again, Alex motioned for the beautiful brunette steward-ess. She leaned in towards him while he whispered something in her ear. A few seconds later, she glanced in my direction with a small, but enticing smile. She then proceeded over to Robert and I.

She placed her hand on mine and spoke seductively, her intentions crystal clear, "Mr. Reuben has asked me to make you very comfortable."

Any man who possessed morals not as strong as myself, would have jumped at such an invitation by this lovely woman. I knew Alex was fully aware I was happily married. Was he testing me or did he simply have no morals of his own? Probably not, a man of his wealth and stature did not know or care about commitment. Regardless of how tempting the offer was or how many drinks I had in my system at this point, I knew right from wrong.

"Rebecca, is it? You are very beautiful, but I am happily married to a wonderful woman," I said, trying not to sound rude.

Rebecca did not seem affected and gave me an understanding smile, before returning to her duties as a stewardess. Alex pretended to take no notice of my rejection, while Robert was completely passed out at this point. Jason and Carter kept to themselves in the front of the plane, very suspiciously I might add. They talked only to each other and paused every few minutes, as if to see if anyone was eavesdropping. Carter continually glanced back at me with an angered look on his face.

It seemed as though the two of them were discussing me. But, what could it possibly be about? I had just met these men, why did they appear so angry? Perhaps I was just over-analyzing the situation. My mind began to wander in an attempt to let this go. It landed back on Dad, the day before his funeral, and what he had left me in his safety deposit box. On that note, I began to doze off.

Stranger in the Forest

Two days earlier, I hesitantly walked through the double doors of my father's bank. Dad's attorney had given me a key to a safety deposit box. In his will, Dad wanted me to have the contents of the box. I didn't want to be dealing with this now, but I had to respect Dad's wishes.

"Hello, I'm Eric Richards, my father left something for me," I told the bank manager very dryly, holding up the key to the box.

The manager spoke, trying to comfort me, "I'm so sorry for your loss, Mr. Richards. Quite frequently we have to empty our lock boxes after the death of its owner. It never seems to get easier."

Without another word, he got up from behind his desk and began to lead me to the safety deposit box. We walked down a long hallway. At the end, the room containing secrets from all over Philadelphia, was sealed by a heavy metal gate.

"Your father had this box for over thirty years," the bank manager remarked, while opening the gate.

He took me right to Dad's box, number 238. He inserted his master key in the first lock, then my key in the second lock. As if he had done it a million times before, the manager took out the small box and placed it on the table in front of me.

"I'll be just down the hall, Mr. Richards, if you need anything else. Take your time."

I stared at the box for what seemed like an eternity, wondering what could possibly be inside for nearly thirty years. Holding my breath, I slowly opened it. Inside, laid a small and very old necklace. It was in mint condition, a circle carved out of some kind of white stone. I knew it had to be ancient because of the language inscribed on the outer rim, which I did not recognize. A cross in the middle of the pendent was surrounded by this language. Where did he get this? Underneath the necklace was a letter from Dad.

It read, "Dear Eric, my only son, I fear that by the time you read this, it will be too late for me. I will have passed on to what I hope will be a far better place than this. I'm not sure what is wrong with me. I seem to be losing my mind, ever since that event. I am remembering only bits and pieces and have been keeping a journal in an effort to remember what I can. Take this necklace that I found years ago. There is something very special and yet very powerful surrounding it, the likes of which I do not understand. I know it is very important, as they are willing to kill to get their hands on it. I love you son. Have faith that I will always be watching over you. Love, Dad."

When I was younger, my father never talked much about himself or the hard times he had been through. So, it was no surprise he had not mentioned this. I continued to analyze the necklace and wondered who 'they' were, he referred to in his letter. What was the 'event'? There was no time to decipher his cryptic message now, I put the necklace and letter in the breast pocket of my suit and walked out of the room.

Not more than an hour after we landed in Brazil, we had our equipment and luggage unpacked. We were at an abandoned air strip, something that seemed to confuse Robert, but I knew better than to question this.

"This place wasn't on any of the maps!" Robert said, hungover from the alcohol-filled flight.

The area was calm and quiet, there was no sign the air strip had been manned in years. So many causes for concern entered my mind as I glanced around the tarmac, bordered by the Brazilian jungle. I had to bite my tongue to suppress my thoughts and uphold the 'no questions asked' policy.

Alex stood on a platform next to some large fueling tanks and addressed everyone, "Gentlemen, please gather around. I want you all to know that there is plenty of fuel in these tanks. I took the liberty of having some friends of mine with the Brazilian government fill them. So you don't think of me as too much of a tyrant, I want you all to take tonight off and relax. Tomorrow, we begin our mission and we won't stop until it has been completed."

He began pointing around the area and continued, "We have fabricated some shelters for your use. The office has been set up already. We had a small crew install power and phone lines prior to our arrival."

The camp made quite an impression on me. For being in the middle of the jungle, it seemed to be rather luxurious, in the typical style of Alex Reuben. However, there was always that one person that couldn't help but complain. I was standing right next to him.

"Too bad we couldn't have gotten some air conditioning set up too," the man mumbled.

I couldn't help myself, I had to say something, "What do you think this is? Some kind of country club? Be a man."

With this, everyone quietly chuckled at the expression on the man's face. It was priceless. My men and I were accustomed to conditions much worse than the Brazilian jungle. To us, Alex's camp was a five-star hotel.

The para military men secured a perimeter around the camp. The rest of the crew began claiming their tents for the night. I tossed my luggage in one at random and couldn't help but stare at the cot. All I wanted to do was sleep, it had been such a long week, and my tent looked pretty cozy at this point. I had to call Sara though and tell her I had made it here safely. She would never let me forget it if I missed a routine check-in.

I found Robert three tents down from mine, "Hey, I'm headed up to the office to call Sara."

Of course he had something smart to say, "That woman's still got you on a short leash, huh?"

"And your wife doesn't?" I remarked.

"Nope, she trusts me."

Ironically, Robert was the last man who should be trusted by a woman. Traveling to another country without his wife was risky, only she didn't know that. I swept his remark about Sara under the rug and proceed up to the office, which was guarded by two men with machine guns.

"Hold it right there. What's your business?" one of the men said, haltingly putting his hand on my chest.

"I just need to call my wife," I said innocently.

"Alright," he said, stepping aside.

That was strange. Why the heavy security on an office, of all things? I reminded myself again, no questions. This policy was getting on my nerves already and it was only the first day. I quickly found the satellite phone and called my wife, relieved and comforted when I heard her voice.

"Sara, honey, how is everything going up there? I miss you and the kids already."

"Eric! We miss you too! The boys are great, your mother is watching them for a while. She decided they would be a good distraction."

As much as I tried, I couldn't disguise the concern in my voice, "How is Mom?"

Sara paused, then said, "She's okay, as well as to be expected. She's still working on cleaning up the house. I hope the boys are helping her. She insisted on going shopping for furniture, probably just to take her mind off of Fredric."

"Well, whatever works for her, I guess. And how are you, darling?"

"I'm fine, Eric. I just wish you didn't have to leave at such a difficult time. It's hard enough dealing with everything that has happened, you being gone makes it worse."

71

"I know, I'm sorry. I had no choice though and we need the money. I'll make it up to you, I promise."

My eyes were beginning to fill with tears, "Just take care of our family and tell the boys Daddy loves them. I'll be home as soon as I can, I love you Sara."

"Love you too Eric. Please be safe. You know how I worry about you every time you're gone."

"I'll be fine honey. Talk to you soon, bye."

God, I missed her so much. Since we had met, we had been inseparable. Being away from each other for my job never got easier. Sara and my mother were always a lot alike. They always worried and stressed over anything they found reason too, like somehow that would uncover a solution. I realized early on, there was no use in trying to ease their troubles, just accept it. I laughed to myself, thinking about how much this had irritated my father.

As I proceeded out of the office, the security guards watched me like a hawk. The rest of the crew had congregated in the large tent in the middle of the camp. I had apparently missed the call for dinner. I entered the dining hall to find a massive spread of decadent meats, cheeses, fruits, and vegetables. This was by far the best looking camping food I had ever seen. I quickly took my place in line and began to cram as much as I could onto my plate, I was famished. Grabbing an Evian bottle at the end of the table, I glanced around at the crew and found Robert at the far table by himself.

I sat next to Robert. My fellow crew members, Lance and Jeff, followed me. Lance was a timid man, not much of a conversationalist, but one hell of a mapper. He was an extremely hard worker and I had deep respect for the man. Jeff, the youngest of the crew, had his strength in the handling of artifacts. He was a bit arrogant and sometimes downright stubborn, but a genius in his own right. The four of us began discussing the upcoming excavation.

Of course Alex and his men were nowhere to be seen. They probably had their own private cabana to dine in. Strangely, Alex had a way of making my stomach turn, so I jumped at the opportunity to relax and have some fun with my crew.

"See what I don't get," said Jeff, scratching his head, "is why all the security?"

"Not to mention getting all the charts and location of the dig today," added Lance.

"It does seem to be either very unprofessional or extremely secretive," said Robert.

I didn't like where this was going and I didn't want to see any of these men reamed by Alex. No one had bothered to inform the rest of the crew of the policy, apparently that job had been left up to me.

Trying to be nonchalant on the matter, I explained, "Guys, we're being paid a lot of money for this, I think the least we could do is not question the man writing our checks. We dig and then we go home, no questions asked. Fair?"

Robert, Lance, and Jeff all nodded in agreement and then quickly left the conversation behind us. We continued talking about everything under the sun, excluding our job. It mostly consisted of the best ways to spend the money we would soon be getting. All I could think about was showering Sara and the boys with anything they could possibly want.

Darkness was fast approaching and our wake-up call the next morning would come even faster. Moaning in pain over eating way too much, we all made our way to our sleeping quarters and promptly fell fast asleep.

Sounds of quads and engines filled the air the next morning. Most of the crew were still half asleep, trying to get their equipment together and chugging coffee at the same time. The sun was barely up and a full day of hard work was ahead of us.

"Alright, men, let's get things rolling! It should only take us a couple hours to get set up at the site." I shouted, in an attempt to wake them up.

Robert was in a particularly good mood. Like a scene from a movie, he popped a cigar in his mouth, cranked up the volume on his cassette player and said, "Let's get paid."

Being somewhat superstitious, this was Robert's usual routine. Jeff couldn't help but laugh as we jumped on our four wheelers and headed for an old trail left by inhabitants before us. Lance, being the expert with the maps, led the way, followed by myself, and then the rest of the crew. We raced down the trail, deep into the jungle, at almost reckless speeds.

Meanwhile, back at camp, Alex's gunmen stood at attention in front of the office. Jason and Carter stepped outside, followed by Alex. All was silent.

Then, Alex addressed his men, "You all know the drill! As soon as they find that temple, destroy it. Then I want you to kill them all. No witnesses!"

"Sir, this won't be as clean as when we poisoned the ship's crew years ago. It's going to be more complicated," observed Jason.

"We will have to use them," answered Alex, pointing to the group of armed soldiers.

Carter interjected in his usual forceful tone, "You know, there's no time for a full transformation of that many people."

"There's no time for this, I trust you will do what needs to be done. Now follow them, don't let anyone out of your site. Move out!" concluded Alex.

Back on the trail, we were getting closer to the site. Being the rainforest, the condition of the trail was deteriorating fast, as the quads kicked up roost behind us. The sun had risen and was beating down on the earth. Everyone, including myself, was focused on the task at hand, completely unaware of the plans devised back at camp.

The jungle heat was beginning to show its fury. I raised my hand, halting everyone to take a break and hydrate. Thankfully, the rainforest canopy was shielding some of the intense rays of sun. Rather than drink the water, I was half tempted to pour it all over my face. Some men did just that, and at the same time, became aware of their agonizing arm pump due to the rough terrain. The majority of the crew were inexperienced in riding, and I firmly believed some would make it to the site faster if they walked.

I stood up on my four wheeler and motioned to everyone break time was over. We continued on. The grips on the handlebars were beginning to give me blisters and sweat was seeping in. Wearing heavy mechanic's gloves could not mask the intensity of the rutted trail. Despite being somewhat uncomfortable, I reveled in the adrenaline. The men unfortunate to be behind me, were getting a face full of mud.

Alex, not surprisingly, had changed the plan late last night, and we were to go straight to the temple. All interest in the ship had been thrown to the wayside when they had finally discovered the exact location of the ancient structure, which was still nowhere to be seen.

If the map was right, we should have been right on top of the location. I had no reason to doubt Lance's abilities though. I came to an abrupt stop and hollered at Lance ahead of me to stop too. The rest of the crew followed, dismounting their quads and taking off their helmets and goggles.

"What's going on?" Lance shouted, looking back at us and holding up his hands in confusion.

"This is the end of the trail!" I shouted back.

Lance pointed to the cliff just a few yards ahead, "We've got a waterfall, and the structure should be down below on the other side."

"Anyone have any ideas of how to get to it?" asked Robert, presenting the obvious question.

Although a slight complication, I knew we could overcome it, "The water seems to be shallow enough, and we should be able to carry our equipment across. We did bring ropes and repelling gear, we can make it down."

I saw almost every man cringe when I mentioned repelling, not our favorite thing to do.

"Once we're down, we can make a line to the other side to get the rest of our things down," I continued.

It seemed simple enough, but we were an excavation team, not a group of mountain men. Wasting no time, we began to gear up and unloaded all the ropes we had. Jeff, being the showoff he often was, took the liberty of repelling first. Once he had reached the bottom and gave the all clear, the rest of us formed a line, ready to slide down one at a time. I stayed at the top, ensuring each man was properly secured, before letting them repel. In a remote part of the world like this, we had to take extreme precautions.

Twenty-five minutes later, half of the crew were at the water-fall down below, when Carter and Jason arrived. Of course right behind them, stood the gunmen and our tree cutter.

"Nice to see you guys finally made it, not too late to help us out," I said.

I had to laugh at the situation with the cutter.

"As you can see, that cutter isn't going across. We'll have to do this one the old fashioned way."

Robert let out a sigh of relief, thinking if his beloved cutter wasn't going, then neither was he. The man was tough as nails, but when it came to heights, he turned into an eight-year-old girl.

"Hey Robbie! Just because your baby isn't going anywhere, doesn't mean you're off the hook!" said one of the men, laughing while strapping on his harness.

"I know that." was all Robert had to say.

He walked over to the edge and whistled to make the effect more dramatic.

"Quite a distance, isn't it? You're sure these ropes will hold me, Eric?"

"You afraid of heights?" the other crew member continued.

"No, just not a particular fan, that's all," Robert replied.

"No need to worry, Robert, these ropes will hold anyone," I said reassuringly.

With a few more words of encouragement, Robert finally took his turn and very slowly repelled down. Two men were left after him. I systematically checked their harnesses too before giving the okay. Once they stepped over and began their decent, I peeked over the edge. My entire crew was safely below and now it was my turn. I gathered my wits and put my backpack over my shoulders. Trying not to let Alex's men fluster me, I concentrated on securing my harness, then stepped backwards over the edge. I shot them one last look before dropping to the rock floor below.

Once my feet touched the ground, I unhooked my harness and joined the rest of the men in forming a line across the water. The crew slowly started moving our backpacks, tents, and some of the heavier equipment to the other side. We had lowered down as many tools as the ropes and our strength would allow from the top of the cliff. Hopefully, what we had would suffice.

It wasn't my problem to make sure Alex's men made it over the drop-off. Frankly, I hoped they didn't possess enough sense to make it down. Alex himself was nowhere to be seen. He must have stayed behind in his air-conditioned office. It did seem a lot better than sweating in the unforgiving heat. Relief would come soon enough though. During this time of year, rain was expected any time and could last a couple days. We were in a rainforest after all.

In the midst of helping Robert fasten his chainsaw to the cable, I spotted what we had been looking for. Lance was right, it was on the other side of the waterfall. The structure had been consumed by the jungle and vines covered nearly the entire area. I could only see a few stones here and there and we would have walked right past it if we weren't looking for it, making me wonder if anyone else had seen it. This was it. I suddenly became very anxious, excited for a new challenge.

"Alright, men, let's pick up the pace! I want everyone's full cooperation so we can make as much progress as possible with what little daylight we have left. I want to start right away on clearing some of the brush in front of the structure," I said, pointing to the area and going into full boss mode.

Lance came trudging through the water towards me, "Sir, we're working on getting the last of the heavy pieces across. We should be able to start clearing shortly."

"Good work, Lance, thank you." I replied

We would have to make camp here tonight. Given our position, going back to headquarters would be time consuming. Alex had made very clear the urgency of this dig.

"And we aim to please," I thought sarcastically to myself.

It was still very exciting to unearth yet another historical find, especially one shrouded in mystery like this. However, the mystery would have to wait until morning. The overgrowth surrounding the structure was so thick, it took longer than expected to even make a dent. I discovered using a machete by hand was the most effective, and yet very crude, way to go. We worked nonstop, ignoring the men with guns standing behind us, until we lost the last of our light.

Darkness descended, engulfing everything, while the temperature began to slowly drop. We had our tents set up in a line cascading up the bank. It was difficult to find an area devoid of rocks. Where we made camp, I could still feel small stones protruding through my sleeping bag. It was difficult to sleep, given the uncomfortable surface. I concentrated on the soothing sound of the waterfall next to us, which thankfully silenced the sound of wild creatures in the night.

Sleep came and went all too quickly. The majority of us were too excited for what we might find in the ruins. The cutting and clearing of trees commenced early. It was a routine now, we would do all the work and Alex's men would stand statue behind us, guns in hand. They showed no emotion while they watched every move we made.

"Lance, can you find me an opening? I'll get started at the entrance here with the jack hammer," I said.

Lance turned off his saw and motioned to his left, "Go over there, about twenty feet and you'll find a clearing. That should be the farthest breach inside. I'll get some more fuel for the saws."

I made my way in the direction Lance had instructed with a shovel and saw, just as the rain started. It started as a drizzle, then within minutes, turned into a downpour. Half the crew stopped what they were doing and frantically hurried to get their sifters and stations covered. I paid no attention to the chaos, I knew my men could handle the situation. I picked up my saw and began clearing brush at the entrance.

Robert, always being the man to step up when the moment was urgent enough, started shouting out orders, "Hurry up! We need supports up in the area where Eric is before we end up with a cave-in!"

"We're on it, Sir!" one of the men yelled back.

I was making progress on the entrance fairly quickly, patience was not my strong point. What could be in there? I noticed the gap becoming more precarious with each motion of my shovel. Just as I was about to cease all work, two of my crew members arrived, posting up bars on each side of the entrance. I knew it was Robert who had been looking out for me. He knew my tendency to get wrapped up in the moment and unconsciously put my own safety on the back burner.

The rain had settled and was falling at a moderate pace. The face of the structure was nearly cleared and the entrance was now stable. It was early in the afternoon and the time had come to venture inside.

"Let's start setting up some light so we can get inside. Good work, men!" I told my crew.

While a small group had been securing and lighting the entrance, the rest of the crew had been gathering pieces of the rubble. They were then sorted out and placed in a specified bin. At a location like this, everything had to be treated as an artifact until proven otherwise. Jeff noticed some of the pieces had a strange writing on them.

He rushed over to me at the entrance, "Eric, wait, hold on!"

"What is it?" I asked, not wanting to be interrupted.

Jeff seemed more concerned with the stones he was carrying than his own safety. He rushed inside the beginning of the opening to meet me, not bothering to put on any protective gear. When Jeff got excited about an artifact, we knew better than to stand in his way.

"Can you bring these pieces out in larger chunks? You're busting them up into pebbles before I can look at them. There some kind of ancient writing on them," he said urgently

"I'll do my best, but according to Alex, the goal is to get inside, and I'm almost there," I told Jeff, he didn't seem happy with my response.

Jeff mumbled something under his breath and crawled out of the cave we had made. We had gone as far as we could before literally hitting a wall. The entrance was just big enough to crawl through, one person at a time. We had to somehow bring in heavy equipment to break through what appeared to be the final wall. I exited the cave and gathered my men to form a game plan, it was a good time to take a break anyways. We were exhausted.

Beyond the clouds, a small glow of light broke through. The glow was unexplainable and not that of the sun. It cascaded into the rain, shining off the canopy as it rapidly traveled to the earth below, impacting on the hillside behind the ancient structure. It was best described as a comet, with a white center and a blue trail being left behind itself. The harmless rain shower had since turned into a menacing storm. The thunder, however, failed to disguise the impact of the object on the ground. It hit not too far north of the ruins and shook the ground.

The force caused the wall in front of me to break and crumble open. What was that? Perhaps an earthquake? Every man next to me had the same confused look on their face. All was silent. We stared at the ancient structure, wondering how to proceed, as the storm lifted. Curiosity got the best of me.

"I have to see what's inside," I told my crew.

The space was not meant for someone who had claustrophobia. I knew it wasn't the brightest idea, the entrance was still in no condition to be crawling through. Luckily, enough lighting had been set up, I could see all the way through. Lance and two other men, against their better judgment, entered the tunnel to check the stability of the supports. Robert insisted on checking them himself too, he would have the final word.

"Careful Eric," was all Robert said as he made his way out of the tunnel, giving me the go ahead.

I put my headlight on and grabbed an extra flashlight, while Jeff handed me a tape recorder. For extra precaution, Robert insisted I take a radio and tie myself to a rope, so I could be fed through the tunnel. I obliged, assuming it was so I could find my way back out. After all, it wouldn't do much good if there was a cave-in.

I took a deep breath, thinking of Sara and the kids, and crawled into the tunnel. I moved at a steady pace, being extra careful not to hit the walls or the ceiling. It didn't matter how many supports had been placed inside, the structure was ancient and unstable. Like any artifact we had ever discovered, this too needed to be handled with care.

I reached the end of the tunnel and the end of our lighting we had installed. Feeling my way around I felt a drop off and slowly lowered one of my legs down until my foot touched the ground. I pulled out my other leg, stood up, and switched on my headlight. Before I went any further, I knew I had to document this, so I took out my tape recorder and began to speak into it.

"This is Eric Richards on the second day of Cove Corporation's expedition in Brazil. Some kind of earthquake has given me access to the inside of some ancient ruins we have found. My team and I were brought here to this temple, to find something of great importance to Alex Reuben. The room I'm standing in is very large from what I can tell. If not for my headlight, I wouldn't be able to see an inch in front of my face."

While I was exploring the temple inside, outside, orders were being thrown out left and right. Lance and Jeff were stopped in their tracks, staring at each other, wondering what to do next. Carter and Jason seemed to be in a panic after the unexplained light fell from the sky. They had taken control of the crew.

"Jason, we need to get in there now," Carter said hastily.

"I know. It's one of them I just know it!" Jason replied.

"It might be, that's why we have to move now. We can't let them interfere again."

Accepting Carter's answer, Jason turned to his men behind them, "I want half of you with me. The rest of you, head up the hill,"

Robert was getting anxious, sensing the intensity of Alex's men. He knew something was wrong and had waited long enough. He rushed to the entrance and shined a spotlight through the small gap.

"Eric, are you okay?" he shouted, with a full measure of worry in his voice.

"Yeah, I'm fine! You should see this, it's amazing, writing everywhere!" Eric shouted back.

Robert crouched next to the entrance, trying desperately to see the other side of the gap. Even with a spotlight, it was far too dark. If Eric was not able, Robert was to assume seniority and lead the crew. He knew exactly what to do.

"Alright, Eric, I'm going to grab some guys and try to widen the gap. We need to get in there and take pictures. Hang tight!"

Lance and Jeff had gone back to cataloging the pieces of ruble that had writing on them. Some of the crew began snapping pictures of the exterior, others cleared the last of the brush, and the rest monitored the entrance and held the rope. The men sorting through the rocks were interrupted at the sound of the gunmen running up the hill.

"Should we go up there too?" Lance asked Jeff.

"Don't even think about it. Get back to work and keep your mouth shut," Jason said, placing his hand on Lance's chest.

Lance complied, not wanting to stir up a fight. The last thing he wanted was to be thrown off the project.

"Everyone, keep working! We have the situation under control!" Jason continued.

At the same time, just up the hill, the soldiers for hire approached the location of the impact. They discovered a sizable crater and were shocked by the glow coming off the center. The leader of the army motioned to the others to disperse off in a circle around the object.

As the men followed his orders, the commanding soldier bent down on one knee to observe the strange substance covering the surrounding trees. He ran his hand along the residue, wondering what it could possibly be. It was a very thin, gelatin-like substance, which seemed to emanate heat. It was so hot, when the rain made contact, steam rose up the side of the trees.

The army was unaware of what their commanding officer had discovered. They were too mesmerized by the glowing object they were now staring at. It was almost too bright to look at, but as they did, it began to slowly move. As it moved, the brightness faded, and a mist began to manifest. What appeared out of the mist was both stunningly beautiful and eerily haunting.

A figure of a completely unclothed woman stood before them. She had long, white, flowing hair and flawless skin. Her eyes were crystal blue and seemed to look directly into your soul.

She appeared to shimmer as her body continued to emit a light glow.

One of the men was completely drawn to her beauty and started to approach her.

"Are you okay, miss? I'm putting down my gun, we're not going to hurt you," he said.

The man had foolishly taken off his helmet and laid his gun on the ground. There was no expression on the woman's face as she stood up in the crater to face him. A golden white light swirled around her as the rain turned into steam, caressing her skin. Her skin must have been boiling hot, but yet she was unaffected. With one look into her piercing eyes, the feeling of compassion and protectiveness that she radiated, quickly turned into fear.

"Sarav et ca Ba-lac taw nee!" her voice echoed off the trees and the ground began to vibrate.

Her face transformed into anger.

"Oh shit! Everyone hit the dirt!" yelled one of the soldiers, sensing something ominous about to happen.

The woman raised both her hands straight out in front of her. A jolt of lightening exhumed from her fingertips, launching the unarmed man into the air. He landed hard on the ground, ten feet from where he had been standing.

"Fire! Everyone fire!" ordered the man, as he tried to come to terms with what had just happened to him.

The army began unloading their magazines at a rapid pace. There was absolutely no damage to the woman as she was fired upon. The bullets only melted off some kind of force field surrounding her skin. Then without warning, she darted to the left, then the right, at lightning speed. Up one tree, then down another she went.

The men tried desperately to track her, as she disposed of them one by one. The commanding officer, still back in the shelter of the trees, didn't know what to make of the gunfire he heard. He knew something had come from the crater and instinct told him to hide.

He fell to the ground and laid flat on his stomach under some vines. An eerie silence fell on the entire area, making it more difficult not to be heard. He held his breath and looked at the ground in front of him, frozen with fear. A pair of bare feet appeared inches from his right hand. He looked up to see the nakedness of the woman in front of him. She placed one hand on his head and in an instant, everything turned black, as he was rendered unconscious.

The woman stripped the man, taking his shirt and pants to cover herself. She then vanished without a trace, leaving the chaos she had just created behind her.

REVELATIONS

O nly minutes earlier, Robert arrived at the cataloging tables where Lance and Jeff were working. Carter, watching the men like a hawk, had overheard Robert telling them something.

"Eric made it inside, we need to get in there and help him. I want you guys to help me widen the gap," Robert told Lance and Jeff.

Carter was about to approach Robert when he was interrupted by the sound of gunfire on the hill. The remaining soldiers at camp pointed to the flashes of light coming off the hillside.

"Something's wrong," one of the men said.

Carter ignored this, he had little care for these men anyways. He rushed to one of the tents to find Jason unpacking a large case containing two automatic assault rifles and silencers.

"Jason!" Carter said with fierce intensity as he threw open the flap on the tent.

"What?" Jason said, preoccupied with assembling his rifle.

"Jason, it's time. Eric's in, we move now."

"I've been waiting three days to hear you say that," Jason replied with delight.

There was no warning of the carnage about to unfold. Carter and Jason emerged from the tent, fully armed, intent only on eliminating any witnesses. A barrage of bullets and blood flowed in the midst of the wounded and dying. The creek bed turned red as each crew member fell. Alex's soldiers looked on, waiting for orders.

The whistles of their silenced weapons formed a symphony, a song of death and destruction, somewhat beautiful in the twisted madness. Men working at the entrance of the cave had discovered what was happening and began to flee. Carter ordered the soldiers to hunt them down and finish the task.

Not a single soul from Cove Corporation was left standing, as the gun thugs mowed them down in no time. They completed a final sweep of the area to confirm that there were no survivors. The evil deed was finished. However, unbeknownst to the soldiers, the hunters were about to become the hunted.

One of the gunmen moved in to notify Carter and Jason of the situation.

"Sir, our mission is completed, everyone's dead."

"Not everyone," Jason replied, staring at his own gun.

Both men threw their guns to the ground, as the soldiers looked on in bewilderment.

"What's going on guys?" one of the men managed to say.

"Your services are no longer needed gentlemen," Carter said.

Carter's hands began to shake and a force erupted out of his palms. The gunmen started running for their lives, screaming in agony as they caught fire from the inside out. The flames flowed from their eyes and mouth, consuming their body as they dropped to the jungle floor.

"Alright, Jason, let's get inside," Carter said with satisfaction.

Through all the mayhem outside, I was completely oblivious inside the temple. The thick walls prevented any kind of sound from seeping in through the outside. I was still rummaging through the ruins, not exactly sure what I was looking for. I continued on, deeper into the temple, until I discovered the bones of a man in uniform laying on the ground.

"As far as I can tell, this man has been here for quite some time. I don't recognize the uniform he is wearing, perhaps an early soldier's outfit. I have been following the writing on the walls, it seems to cover the entire area inside. It appears to be a mixture of two different languages. One could possibly be Greek, the other I'm not sure of."

I noticed something metallic reflecting underneath the soldier's legs, it was a small three by three inch cube. This must have been what Alex Reuben was searching for. I gently picked up the object and placed it in my pocket.

My tape recorder in my hand clicked off as did my headlight, startling me. While reaching into my pocket for my backup flashlight, I thought of how I wished Sara were here. She would be able to decipher the writings.

The second flashlight was of no use either. I switched it on and it flickered a few times before going dead too. I began to get anxious, it had been far too long since I had any contact with my men outside.

"Hello? Anyone there? Robert?" I said at the sound of footsteps.

Robert had probably made it through the gap and was coming in to take some pictures. The footsteps were getting louder as they drew nearer. They were not the heavy boots of any of my men.

The faint sound of a woman's voice sent chills down my spine, "Tua ar ela sactone bera."

Out of the darkness, two shining blue eyes appeared directly in front of me. As they gazed at me, the necklace my father gave me began to glow a soft white. I had been wearing it during the whole trip and nothing had happened. It got brighter and brighter until the whole room was as bright as the daylight.

The light revealed a beautiful woman that belonged to the brilliant eyes I had just seen.

"Sorry Eric, sometimes I forget when I am speaking with a heavenly tongue," she said.

"What? Who are you? How do you know my name?" I was confused.

Strangely enough, I did not feel threatened or in any danger. This woman had kindness in her eyes. Or was she a woman? How did her eyes shine the way they did?

She spoke softly again, "Eric, there's little time left. I will answer all your questions, but first, we must leave now."

Then, she raised one hand in front of my chest and my necklace began to lift up in the air. A palpable energy began to swirl around us as the medallion hovered in front of my very eyes, still connected to the chain around my neck.

"Eric, you must take the necklace, hold it firmly in your hand," the woman instructed.

She could see my hesitation and added, "No need to worry, please trust me."

Reluctantly, I agreed to do as she said. I didn't really have a choice and there was no telling what she could do to me if I declined. I reached out in front of me and grasped the levitating medallion. The energy became stronger.

At the same time, the woman grabbed both my shoulders and said, "This may be very cold and hurt a little."

The unusual energy traveled in a vortex around us, tingling as it brushed my skin. Ribbons of blue and white light began to form within the vortex and moved at incredible speeds. I was mesmerized by these brilliant colors. Then, a warm wind suddenly manifested and rushed through us. As this happened, the colors slowly faded. The wind then died down and it seemed as though time itself had stopped. All these events had occurred in sheer seconds.

Everything was still when I heard the woman speak to me again, "Are you okay, Eric?"

"It's so cold," I replied, trying to steady my equilibrium.

"Maybe it's because you are face down in the snow. After all, I told you it might be cold. Now get up, we must keep moving."

She placed her right hand on the side of my face and I instantly became warmer.

"That won't last long, we need to get you into some warmer clothes," she said.

I looked down to see I was still wearing my light weight khakis and Cove Corporation t-shirt. I was no longer in Brazil, the temperature had dropped dramatically, and I was surrounded by snow.

"Where are we?" I finally asked, still confused.

"We're at the place you most wanted to be when I transferred my energy to you. You were the one who chose where we would go, I simply supplied the power to get us there."

The event back in Brazil was an energy transfer? I was dazed as I glanced around at my surroundings. I recognized our location immediately, I had been here countless times before. We were in the middle of Michael and David's favorite park in downtown Philadelphia.

The woman I was somehow still following, led me to a clothing store not far away to bundle up in some warmer clothes. As we walked through the door, the man at the front counter stared at us, slightly amused.

"What happened to you two?" he asked

"Don't ask. We just need some appropriate clothing," said the woman, smiling at the clerk.

The man smiled back, eyeballing her because of her stunning beauty. I quickly picked out some clothes and headed for the dressing rooms to change. The woman followed, taking the room next to me. As we changed into our new clothes, she began to explain what had just happened.

"You can call me Anna, by the way. I should have mentioned that a while ago. No, I am not an extraterrestrial being or anything like that."

"What are you then?" I asked with utmost curiosity.

"I believe the term used here on Earth is 'angel'."

I was waiting for more information, she couldn't just say she was an angel and then stop. I had too many questions.

"We need to hurry, Eric. We must get you back home."

I did as she said and we purchased our clothes, exiting the store.

"You have time for one more question on our way back to your house. Then I will answer the rest when I see you in two days," Anna said as we stood on the sidewalk outside the store.

"How do you know me?" It was difficult to choose only one question.

"I have been watching and protecting your family for centuries. Whether you accept it or not, your family is a part of something bigger than you can even imagine. You are in a war that is as old as time itself."

Before I could inquire as to what she meant by that, we had arrived at my house.

"Now listen, Eric, that necklace you have around your neck is the key to everything, as is that object you discovered in the temple. Guard them with your life and tell no one, not even your wife, anything that has happened."

"Anna, I can't keep something like this from Sara!"

"In time, she will be brought into our circle, but not now.

I must go before she sees me."

Before I could utter another word, Anna was gone. I somehow had to come up with an explanation of why I was back so early. Sara was a very inquisitive person and I had to tell her something. There were too many questions and not enough answers swarming my brain, I could barely think.

What the hell was going on? Was I losing my mind? Was I dreaming? Did angels really exist? Did any of my crew notice I vanished in Brazil? I couldn't help but think I would wake up at any minute and be back in a tent at our dig site. Robert would be hung over, complaining about having to work, while Jeff and Lance bickered about whose job was more important.

The snow was falling thick upon the back porch, as it was only weeks from Christmas. I was still trying to figure out what I would say to my wife. Everything, of course, depended on whether Alex Reuben had contacted her when I went missing today. Maybe he didn't even know yet.

I looked through the window and saw Sara smiling, while she decorated the Christmas tree with the boys. Traditionally, we would do this as a family. Through all the craziness in the last few days, nothing could taint this perfect moment I was witnessing.

I held the object in my hand, it was time to go inside. I crept around to the front door, hoping Sara wouldn't notice me yet. I dusted the snow off my jacket and slowly opened the door before running upstairs. Hiding the necklace and artifact was my number one priority and I knew exactly where to conceal them, my wall safe behind our family picture from last Christmas. The necklace and object were still cold to the touch from being outside. I placed the object in the safe, then gazed at the necklace one more time, wondering how it possessed such mystical powers. Then, I sealed both away in the safe.

So as not to create more questions, I carefully went back down the stairs and out the door. Then I pretended as though I was coming back home for the first time.

"Honey?" I called for Sara.

"Eric! Is that you?" she was surprised.

I walked into the living room where the boys were meticulously decorating the tree. A wonderful aroma of freshly baked apple pie filled my nostrils and brought back a flood of memories from holidays past. It was good to be home.

Michael and David abandoned the Christmas tree when they saw me and rushed over to greet me. I threw my arms around both of them, holding them tight.

"Daddy, we missed you! Look at what Michael and I did," David said, pointing to the tree and all their handmade ornaments.

"I missed you too, the tree looks beautiful," a lump was beginning to form in my throat, I was so thankful to see my boys again.

"David and Michael have been working very hard and have waited all week to show you their accomplishment," Sara added as she entered the room.

"Eric, I missed you so much. You're home early, aren't you?"

She hugged and kissed me as though I had been gone for years. It certainly felt like that. Releasing me from her loving grips, she gazed at me expecting an explanation for my early arrival. At least this meant no one had contacted her yet. A simple answer should suffice.

"Oh, we just finished up early," I responded as she took the steaming pie out of the oven.

"You should have called to tell me. None of the boys from your team called either," Sara continued.

"We were in such a hurry to complete the dig, Alex Reuben ran a tight ship. Sorry honey, I should have told you."

She seemed to accept my answer. David and Michael ran into the kitchen, insisting on some pie and vanilla ice cream. I took the same and then we all sat down as a family at the table, Sara was eager to hear about my trip. The boys were more focused on their desserts.

"How was the dig?" she asked.

I told her only what she needed to know. Being surrounded by armed gunmen, in the middle of a remote jungle, in the pouring rain was probably not something she would like to hear. I wanted so desperately to tell her about Anna, but I cut the conversation short. That didn't get past Sara though, she knew I was hiding something.

Luckily, she seemed to quickly let it go and said only one thing, "I'm glad you guys had a productive time down there."

If only she knew about the languages I had seen in the ruins, or the object I had hidden upstairs, she would go absolutely crazy. She loved archeology, and most of all, extinct languages. She had even turned this into a career in teaching. Her passion for archeology and my obsession for being the first to discover a new site is what had bonded us together in the first place. I wondered how long I could hide everything from her. It was not how we maintained our marriage, we told each other everything.

We followed the boys back to the living room. They were adamant about finishing up their decorating duties. Sara and I sat on the couch, watching our kids and enjoying each other's company. It was always difficult spending time apart, even a week seemed like forever.

I would be meeting Anna in two days at the same park. Hopefully, I would get some answers, not more questions.

Sara softly nudged me in the ribs with her elbow, "Should I put a movie on for the kids?"

Her voice was warm and tender as her long hair cascaded over my shoulder.

"Sure, that sounds like a good idea," I replied.

She jumped off the sofa and began to shuffle through the wide array of tapes next to the T.V.

"Hey honey, I'm going to run upstairs and take a quick shower. I'll be back down in a few minutes."

"Okay, you must be needing one anyways. I didn't want to say anything Eric, but I could smell you from the hallway when you walked in," Sara said smiling, clearly amused.

"Oh, very funny," I replied and kissed her on top of the head, before heading upstairs.

The hot water fell soothingly upon my face, washing away days of sweat and dirt from Brazil. It was surreal being back home, but I couldn't shake the unbearable feeling of being lost without any control or direction.

For some reason, I felt compelled to take the necklace from the safe and put it back around my neck. It gave me a sense of security having it on me. My father had clearly known the importance of it, according to his letter, but who was it that was willing to kill for it? Had Dad really been murdered because of it?

I continued to stare at the small stone, which to me, still seemed like just a necklace. As I watched the water bead down the stone, I heard a faint noise of something hitting the floor outside of the shower.

"Sara? Can you pass me a towel, hun?"

With no response, I pulled back the shower curtain. I was suddenly frozen with fear. In the mirror, I saw a dark figure of a man. It had no face, only a hooded cloak revealing black, eyes.

"Your mine!" it shouted.

Then, in the blink of an eye, it was gone. I was so startled, I slipped and landed on the floor of the bathtub.

Sara heard the loud thud and knocked on the door, "Are you okay in there?"

"Yeah, I'm fine," although I was not.

What the hell was that? It had to be stress and exhaustion. I hadn't slept since I left Brazil and now I was starting to hallucinate. I collected myself, examining some minor scrapes inflicted from my fall, and pulled a towel around my waist.

"Are you alright?" Sara asked as I came out of the bathroom.

"I'm okay, just a little tired," I replied.

"I heard a loud bang, did you fall?" she was persistent as she passed me my pajamas.

"Just a little slip, I think I need some rest."

"Okay, honey, I love you," she said and kissed me on the cheek.

I wasn't even completely dried off before I collapsed on the bed. I could hear Sara in the bathroom brushing her teeth.

Between gargles of toothpaste I heard her say, "I'll be up in a little while. Don't worry about the kids, I'll get them to school. You stay home and sleep, I'm worried about you."

Not long after those words left her lips, I was passed out on the bed.

It was nearly noon the next day when I awoke from my deep slumber. I spent the rest of the day lounging around the house, playing with the boys, and visiting with Sara. An endless parade of unanswered questions invaded my mind. It didn't matter what I did, I was distracted all day and Sara was beginning to notice.

How do I explain to Alex or my team why I left the project? Why had no one from the crew called my house when I went missing? I had to find out for myself. The next day, I decided to call Robert's wife to see if he had made it home yet.

Grace picked up on the second ring.

"Hi Grace, its Eric. Is your husband there?"

"No, I haven't heard from him. Are you home?" she asked, completely confused why I would be back and not the others.

I quickly fabricated another lie to cover the mountain of lies I had already created.

"I got sick while I was down there, so Jeff took over for me and I came home."

Although I was still bewildered as to why the rest of the guys wouldn't be home yet, let alone call to check in. Would they just continue with the project after they noticed I was gone? I was pretty sure I had the object Alex Reuben was searching for in my possession. It stood to reason everyone would return after coming up empty-handed.

"Please call me, Eric, if you hear anything from Robert. It's not like him to go this long without checking in."

"I will, I promise. Take care, Grace."

Nothing was adding up. Something was definitely wrong.

I thought of how much trouble I would be in if Alex discovered I had the object. I didn't understand what use it could be to him. However, judging from Alex's actions in Brazil, I knew there was no reason he wouldn't want something of such historical significance.

I had only a half hour until I had to meet Anna at the park. I checked once more to make sure the object was secure in the safe and that the necklace was still around my neck. With each passing day, it was becoming clear that Dad had died because of these two items. I wasn't about to let anything happen to them.

I left Sara a note on the kitchen counter, so she wouldn't worry about me when she got home from work. Then, I made my way outside to my jeep, which was parked next to the sidewalk. The old beast never ran right when the temperature dropped and it took nearly five minutes to get it started.

Before meeting Anna, I had to make one stop at the bank to see if the initial payment for the Brazil contract had been deposited into my account. The teller checked my balance and noticed the surprised look on my face when she told me the payment had been made. A sum of forty thousand dollars was now sitting in my account. Because of what had happened on the trip, I didn't want the payment revoked, so I pulled out the entire amount and had it placed in our safety deposit box.

Walking out of the bank, a thought suddenly entered my mind about the medallion around my neck. Had Dad met with Anna before? Had he been involved in the 'war' Anna talked about?

The lights glimmered and shined off the streets and sidewalks, as Christmas shoppers clambered by the store front windows. The beauty of the holiday season was mixed with the stress of last minute shopping. Frigid temperatures kept most people indoors. Even the Santa suit-wearing volunteer fundraiser decided to take his bell and bucket into the nearest store.

Traffic downtown was a nightmare as usual. Attempting to navigate through the city center on the way to the park was enough to drive a sane person mad. Vehicles refusing to start in the extreme cold were abandoned on the side of the road.

Despite all the distractions, I made decent time. I parked my vehicle at the curb and then glanced in my rear view mirror. The effects of the past few weeks were visible all over my face. I grimaced at my haggard appearance.

Anna, the beautiful angel with glistening white hair, was waiting for me. Looking through the fogged up windshield, I recognized her perfect figure. A gentle peace came over me at the site of her. It was almost as though she could make everything right again. This feeling, perhaps, came from her telling me she had been watching over me for years now.

I looked down to make sure my jacket was securely buttoned and noticed my necklace was glowing softly again. I got out of the jeep and walked over to meet her.

Before I could even properly greet her, she motioned for us to go back to the vehicle, rather than out in the open. I obliged and we walked back. I started up the beast once again and let the heater permeate the interior.

"I have not fully descended yet," Anna began.

I was not sure what she meant by that, then she proceeded to explain herself further.

"Listen very carefully to me Eric," she began.

Having a conversation with an angel, you would think there wouldn't be any doubt in my eyes. I would be hanging on her every word.

"I should be fully descended in a day or two. Until then, it is not wise for me to be around you."

"Why?" I interjected.

"Don't interrupt, just listen! Until I am descended, they can sense my presence. It is not my safety I am concerned about, it's yours. Those men who hired you are not who they appear to be. They are pure evil, soldiers of the man you call Alex Reuben. Here on Earth, they are known as demons. The bodies they inhabited are not their own and were taken over by fallen angels."

"Over sixty years ago..." she continued on.

I listened intently, finding it difficult to believe in the history she was telling me. Alex Reuben's men didn't age like the rest of us. Alex himself, was at least a thousand years old. How could we hope to defeat something that had century's worth of experience?

Anna must have been able to read my thoughts as she responded to them right away, "Your job isn't to win this war."

She placed her hand on mine, reassuring me, with kindness in her eyes.

"I'm here when you absolutely need me to help, but I can't be everywhere. Soon, I will teach you as much as I can, to protect yourself and your family."

Anna then went on to tell me about six other chosen families, who were even stronger than mine, that died for this cause.

"Your father was among the many brave individuals."

"My father? What about my father?" I asked.

"He was killed for what he had stumbled upon in Brazil. Did you think all these things that happened were a coincidence?"

At this, a massive amount of anger began to rise inside of me. I was no longer processing her words. I was hell-bent on knowing the identities of my father's killers.

"Tell me who it was!" I yelled, my voice ringing through the cab.

"I won't," Anna said, in a calming tone.

She seemed to look into my soul, then added, "The heart of revenge will only blind you from what you are meant to do. You need to let go. That road will only lead to more suffering. If you choose to pursue it, you will let your father's death and countless others be in vein."

She then spoke of love, "Perfect love casts out all fear and anger. How many foolish men have died at the hands of its clutches?"

My heart rate was decreasing as I finally came down from my cloud of anger.

"I didn't ask for this. What if I simply refuse to be a part of it?" I asked.

"Eric, you can't ignore your destiny."

"I don't even believe in Him." I hoped that would somehow change her mind.

"He believes in you, and so do I. I have faith in you, Eric Richards."

"So that's it then? What do I have to do?"

With that, I lit up another cigarette. I wasn't even a smoker, but had felt the need to purchase a pack on my way to the park. All this talk of destiny nonsense would drive any man to smoke.

Waiting for me to ignite the roll of tobacco, Anna finally said, "Just survive. At all costs, you must live. In three days, I will return to take you to a training ground. There, you will learn to defend yourself against this evil. These demons will catch up to you eventually. It's my job to make sure you are ready for that when the time comes."

She reached for the door handle, "I have to go now."

"Wait!" I snapped, putting out the half smoked cigarette, "What now? How will I find you?"

She paused outside of the jeep, then walked over to my side, motioning to open the door.

She leaned in and whispered in my ear, "I'll find you. Until then, continue to love your family."

Anna closed the door and walked into the park. As she went through the trees, a white flash of light emanated from the branches. Within seconds, she was gone.

The words she had spoken resonated in my mind. The way her voice changed when she told me to love my family had sent chills down my spine. It was as though I wouldn't see their faces for a very long time. The thought nearly made me ill.

I slowly made my way back to the house, being careful not to hit any patches of ice. I came to a stop at the light, the snow was beginning to fall heavily. I watched the wiper blades move back and forth, mesmerized by the repetition. In that moment, I realized how much Dad had given up to protect his family. He had driven himself mad in an effort to conceal the secret.

I remembered how Anna had told me that no matter what, I could not run from my destiny. Is that what happened to Dad? He had hid the necklace, hoping that would stifle anymore events. But despite his efforts to end whatever this was, the demons had destroyed his mind. Despite Anna's cautionary words, I would make whoever killed him pay for what they did.

The streets began to die down as the shops prepared to close for the night. I finally arrived at the house. Shutting off the vehicle, I walked up the stone path to the front door. I found Sara playing with David and Michael on the living room floor. I knew I would do whatever it took to protect them.

THE ACCUSATION

Across town, FBI Agent Carla Munoz was sitting at her desk, analyzing pictures from Fredric Richards' case. She was eager to solve the old man's murder. She grew increasingly irritated at the lack of reliable leads as the case dragged on.

"Have we gotten the autopsy report back on the doctor's body?"

Munoz's partner, Darren Walker, handed her the pathology results.

"What's this suppose to mean? They're inconclusive!" Carla was irate.

She continued, "The man's brain can't just liquefy without a cause. I've never seen anything so gruesome, and I've seen a lot!"

"At least we know the man was dead before he was thrown out the window. The same was done to Fredric, his brain turned to jelly as he sat in his chair," Darren responded.

"The people who did this were some sick bastards!" Carla rested her head in her hands, completely dumfounded.

"We still have the sketch from one of the hospital's staff members," Darren was trying to shed some light.

Carla was not satisfied with this. The sketches provided by the eye witness were very vague and of little help. According to the witness, the two men appeared to be in their early thirties. They were both about six feet tall and wore regular staff uniforms.

"I feel like we are getting nowhere with this. Any longer and the whole case will get shelved for sure."

"Hey Carla, maybe you should use some vacation time. A break might do you some good," Darren said, hoping she wouldn't be angered at the suggestion.

"I think we should just take a break and get something to eat. I'll buy, you drive," Carla's suggestion was better.

Darren was more than delighted to finally be the one to drive. He followed Carla's directions, which led to what looked like a Chinese restaurant. Despite its shady appearance, the interior was actually quite elegant. Carla ordered the chicken teriyaki while Darren opted for sweet and sour pork. The two enjoyed meaningless conversation, something that was a rarity in their line of work.

In the midst of arguing about who had less of a personal life, Carla and Darren were interrupted by the director of the FBI.

"Afternoon Munoz, Walker. You might want to take your lunch to go."

Carla was not happy her lunch break had been ruined, "Why? What's so urgent?"

"There's been a development, I'll fill you in on the way back to the office."

They quickly asked for boxes to pack up their meals. After leaving a sizable tip for the waitress, the two partners were out the door.

Director Williams began the debriefing, "About fifteen minutes ago, we received a package. This package, which came from the office of one Alex Reuben, contained photos of a very graphic, multiple homicide in Brazil. From the photos, we are able to count nearly a dozen victims of this gruesome massacre."

The director began handing out the pictures to his agents gathered around the table. Carla examined the note that came attached to the package.

"Darren, you're not going to believe this. According to Alex Reuben, the person responsible for this atrocity is none other than Eric Richards."

Darren wasn't sure he had heard correctly, "You're joking, right?"

"This is sick," was all Carla could say.

"How could one man create so much carnage?"

Darren was still stunned.

The agents continued to discuss the evidence that had just fallen into their laps, until the director finally interrupted, "Everyone, I want him taken in alive ASAP! Consider him to be likely armed and dangerous. Let's move out!"

"Darren, I want you riding with me," Carla said while strapping on her bullet proof vest.

"Yes, ma'am," Darren was used to being ordered around.

"I want to question him myself," Carla muttered to herself.

The director halted everyone once more, "I want four cars on this and a truck for transport, just in case."

"Why the truck, Sir?" one of the men asked.

"We don't know if Richards had accomplices or not," replied the director.

The agents pealed out from FBI headquarters, on a mission to arrest Eric Richards. Sirens blared down the streets of Philadelphia, as civilians frantically tried to get out of the way. The gloomy December afternoon was suddenly lit up by lights from the police cruisers.

Carla and Darren continued to contemplate the recent development, "Darren, I just can't believe this is the same guy I talked to at his father's funeral. This hardworking family man doesn't seem capable of something so horrible."

Carla desperately tried to put together the pieces of the puzzle, as she stared at the crime scene photos.

Little did I know, my family's quiet afternoon together was about to reach a chaotic conclusion.

Sara was on the phone talking to Mom. I was sitting on the sofa with David and Michael, who were fast asleep in my arms. It was the epitome of a perfect moment.

"Eric, your mother wants to know when you'll be going back to work," Sara asked as she hung up the phone.

In all honesty, I didn't know if I had a job to go back to. All my men were currently unaccounted for and Alex could sue our company for not completing the contract, after what happened in Brazil. I couldn't tell Sara that, and I certainly couldn't tell her I would be meeting with Anna again.

"Soon," was all I could say.

Tomorrow I would begin my special training for a war that I was not responsible for starting. A war that I was somehow now a part of, something I never asked for. I now wished I had never gone to Brazil in the first place. It seemed all hell had broken loose after I discovered that object. Deep down though, I knew it wouldn't have mattered one way or the other. If Anna was right, like I knew she was, this was my destiny and I could not escape it.

I was afraid of failing.

Did it mean my own death if I did fail? I knew I must succeed in protecting my family. Looking at the boys and holding them tightly in my arms, I knew that was motivation enough to defeat the evil. Sara came over and sat next to us. I gazed at her longingly, I loved this woman so much. I would do whatever it took to keep these three safe.

A knock at the door disturbed my thoughts. Sara jumped up to answer it.

"Hello?" Sara said.

Agent Munoz and her partner were standing on the door step. Behind them waited several cars and a transport truck, a worrisome look graced their faces.

"Can I help you?" Sara continued, as she began to sense something was wrong.

"Mrs. Richards, is your husband home?" Munoz was the first to speak.

"Yes, but what's this about?"

With this, Munoz, her partner, and two other agents barged through the door, nearly knocking Sara over and waking up the boys.

"Mr. Richards, you're coming with us," Munoz firmly said.

"What the hell?" I said.

David and Michael were afraid and jumped off the couch, running to Sara. Sara held them in her arms as she looked at me, ready to burst into tears.

"You're under arrest for the murder of your colleagues in Brazil. You have the right to remain silent. If you give up that right, anything you say can and will be used against you in a court of law. If you cannot afford an attorney, one will be appointed to you. Do you understand your rights Mr. Richards?"

"What? They're dead? How? That can't be!" I couldn't believe what was unfolding before my very eyes.

One of the agents grabbed me and checked for any weapons I may have been carrying. I looked at my family one last time and mouthed 'I love you' before they escorted me out of the house. Sara and the kids became emotional.

"Mommy, where are they taking Daddy?" asked David.

Sara followed me out the door, yelling at the detectives. David and Michael stayed in the house, staring out the doorway and crying.

"There must be some mistake! Tell them Eric! My husband is not capable of something like that! You can't take him!" Sara yelled through her sobs, protesting the ridiculous accusation.

The twins then suddenly ran out of the house and latched on to my legs, trying to hold me back. They were crying hysterically.

"You can't take him!" they echoed Sara's words.

Munoz glared at Sara, "Ma'am, would you control your kids!"

It was just days before Christmas and our family was being ripped apart.

The chaos continued onto the front lawn, where Sara frantically pleaded with the agents not to take me. She was thoroughly ignored as I was handcuffed and placed in the truck. Through the small window, I could see our neighbors standing on the sidewalk, staring at the scene unfolding in front of them. Some were in disbelief, while others watched on in horror. I had been living next to these people for years and now they were witnessing me being carted away like a common criminal.

The couple from across the street walked over to Sara in a guise of comforting arms. I knew it was more so to gain information for their gossip circles. It wouldn't be long before the whole neighborhood had enough substance to start constructing rumors.

The woman spoke to Sara, "Are you okay, dear?"

Given the current situation, it was quite possibly the stupidest question to ask. I could see Sara begin to fume at the preposterous inquiry.

"Don't talk to me! Leave me alone!" she responded, then ran inside, dragging the kids back to the house.

Agent Munoz shouted to the others, "I'll follow you back."

With that, a flurry of sirens and lights swept down the street, with me in tow.

A week earlier, the arrest and transport of Eric Richards would have been near impossible due to the massive winter storm that had swept through Philadelphia. On this day however, the streets were clear. There were only a few cars on the road, something very rare, given the time of day.

However, the quietness was about to change dramatically.

The vehicles traveled through the city, en route to HQ for booking and processing. Two cars led the pack and one flanked the truck on each side. Carla Munoz brought up the rear, ensuring maximum security.

Darren, in the cruiser to the left of the truck, radioed Carla, "Munoz, don't you think this is a bit much on the man power?"

"Better safe than sorry. I believe Eric had help and we can't take a chance that one of his accomplices might try to free him. Until that's ruled out, this is the way we are doing things," Carla firmly said.

At the same time, on the fifth floor of an abandoned building, a man with binoculars was looking down at the convoy, about to enter the city center.

The man turned on his radio and said only a few words, "They're arriving now, just off the highway. What are your orders?"

Another dark and sinister voice came through the radio and echoed in the vacant room, "You stay put, we'll handle things from here."

The cars down below were forced into a straight line as they exited the off-ramp. Pure chaos was about to ensue.

Carla watched as the vehicles in front of her flashed their brake lights, reaching a stop sign.

"How's everything going up there?" she asked, wondering why they were moving so slow.

Patience was not her strong suit.

"Everything's good, shouldn't be more than five minutes now," the lead car replied.

Eric, in the back of the truck, continued to shout his innocence. The drivers were growing increasingly more irritated.

"I'm telling you! I've done nothing wrong!"

The man in the passenger's seat told him to shut up.

"If you knew what was good for you Eric, you wouldn't say another word!"

Then all was silent.

Sitting handcuffed in the cold, dark, transport truck, I wondered how my entire crew could be dead. At the thought of Jeff, Lance, and my best friend Robert, I began to cry. At the same time, anger quickly filled my heart.

No, it couldn't be my fault, could it? The assailants were after the artifact, I was sure of it. Alex Reuben and his gun-toting thugs had killed everyone for it. I realized in that moment, that if Anna hadn't been there to save me, I too would be dead. I would have joined my father and my crew members, all for what was now sitting in the safe behind our family portrait. They must have known by now I had what they were looking for.

I suddenly remembered what Anna had told me just days earlier, "They will show no mercy for you or anyone else. They only care about destroying that artifact and they will kill anyone who stands in the way."

The handcuffs were beginning to dig into my wrists. I stared at the grated floor of the truck, trying to focus on anything but the irritation. Anna was an angel, she must have known by now what had happened. Hopefully, she would come looking for me when I didn't show up for our meeting.

In the distance, a man ran along the hard concrete surface of the rooftops, following the convoy below to his right. His pace increased as he jumped from one roof to another, his feet scraping against the unforgiving surface. His black trench coat waved like a flag behind him.

Gliding through the air, it was almost as if he were traveling in slow motion. His stealth like that of an eagle, soaring through the darkening sky. His face was one without emotion and yet extremely focused at the same time. He continued his dance on the rooftops down the street, until he was within yards of the convoy.

One of the agents leading the procession spotted the dark figure above them, "Who's that? Darren, do you see that man hopping the roofs at three o'clock?"

Before Darren could respond, the figure in solid black jumped from the building beside them. He landed on a parked car with such furious impact, the vehicle was completely crushed.

"What in the world?" the radio buzzed.

"Carla, did you see that?"

"There's no way he survived, that's at least twenty stories!"

The sound of bending metal and the crunching of broken glass emanated from the wreckage as the man began to stand up, brushing pieces of debris from his shoulders. He stared directly into the window of the nearest cruiser, his eyes went from grey to black, before returning to normal.

"I don't believe it! Everyone move now!" ordered the boss.

"Too late, we're boxed in," Darren solemnly responded.

Another man wearing all black jumped down from the train trestle in front of them. With a single punch to the air, the man was able to flip the first car upside down. Then with another swift motion of his hands, sent the cruiser and its occupants violently sliding into a nearby building.

The rest of the convoy began to panic, reaching for their holstered guns out of reflex. One agent got out of his car and began firing on the assailant who jumped from the roof. The shots had no effect on the man, as he continued to walk towards the agent, who was frantically emptying his clip. The mystery man then grabbed him by the throat and tossed him over the car, into a storefront window.

"Darren! Darren get out!" Carla cried in horror over the radio.

At this, the man who had jumped from the trestle, set his sights on Carla. He did not break his menacing gaze from her, as he disposed of another agent in his way.

"Oh shit," Carla whispered, as she attempted to flee her car.

She was not fast enough, as the cloaked figure was faster. He clinched his left hand into a fist. Then slowly, his arm turned darker at the shoulder and his hand became brighter. Energy was suddenly discharged from his hand as he punched the passenger side of Carla's car. The impact was like the firing of a cannon. The car, with lightning speed, collided with a parked Mustang on the side of the street. Carla was pinned inside.

Agent Munoz was left with no choice, but to watch in fright, as her partner was targeted next. Darren exited his car, with every intention of fighting them off, but no hope of defeating their wrath. One of the hooded men picked up a gun off the ground and aimed for Darren. Before Darren had a chance to fire a single shot, he collapsed to the pavement.

The sound of the gun rang in the air, combined with Carla's deafening screams. The entire contents of the semi-automatic pistol's magazine were emptied toward Darren.

In the transport truck, I could see the driver was frozen in fear. The dark figures were headed our way.

"Drive dammit!" I shouted at the driver.

The agent hit the gas and slammed right into one of the men in front of us. He was then dragged several feet before his trench coat was ripped off his body. I was somehow not surprised when I saw the man rise to his feet after the truck had released him.

Neither one of the assailants were pleased with this and began to chase us down, despite the fact that we were moving at break-neck speeds. Both men lunged at the truck and latched onto the rear doors, standing on the bumper. With ease, they ripped the doors off their hinges and threw them on the street behind the vehicle.

"Oh God, help me," I said, stunned.

"Not this time Eric, you're coming with us!" one of the men said with pleasure.

This was when I knew how true the words Anna had spoken really were. I began struggling to escape the clutches of the men, but I had nowhere to go. I became more and more tense, and as I did, something else began to happen. My chest started to get warm, almost hot. A white glow became visible from underneath my shirt. This was the same light that always appeared in the presence of Anna. It was my father's necklace.

I stared at the men and shouted, "I'm not going anywhere!"

A beam of brilliant, white light, burned through my plaid shirt, blasting the two men out the back of the truck. They were dead before they even hit the pavement, where their bodies rolled for a few yards and came to a stop.

Their skin was scorched completely black. On the impact of the beam, I saw what looked like the very essence of evil, get blown from their bodies.

The origin of this powerful force was emanating from my necklace. I stared at it, as the light was slowly fading, and wondered how such a thing could be possible. The driver of the truck had come to a stop and both FBI Agents were now staring at me, shocked and speechless.

Carla, still stuck inside her car, finally managed to kicked out the windshield. Crawling out on top of the hood, she immediately ran over to her partner Darren. He was still lying on the ground, his breaths short and broken through his almost lifeless, blue lips.

"You hold on Darren! You stubborn bastard, don't you die on me! Stay with me, help is on the way!" Carla cried hysterically.

She continued yelling at her unresponsive partner until the medics arrived.

Later at headquarters, two agents had shoved me into an isolated cell at the very back of the building. After what had just occurred downtown, they weren't about to take any unnecessary chances.

I had somehow become public enemy number one.

My driver from the transport truck had ordered his fellow officer to watch me very closely.

"Keep a good eye on this one. He's fucking deadly, trust me," he said

Even from the back of the building, I could hear the entrance door slam open and Agent Munoz screamed, "Where is he? I want to see him now!"

My head fell as I waited for the inevitable. I heard the urgent footsteps getting closer, then looked up and saw Munoz staring at me through the bars.

"You better start talking, Mr. Richards. What the hell just happened back there?"

I didn't know what to say. I was just as shocked as she was.

"You better have an airtight alibi concerning the death of your crew and your mysterious disappearance from Brazil."

She continued to study me, waiting for a response. I had nothing.

"You're the only suspect we have. Who were your friends back there? They were helping you escape, why did you kill them?" she was relentless.

At this point, I'd had enough of Munoz's ranting and finally spoke.

"Look, they weren't friends of mine at all.

I don't know who they were. Maybe you should do your job and examine their charred bodies lying on the street."

This only fueled the fire burning in Munoz's eyes.

"Excuse me? I was a little busy tending to my injured partner. He might not make it through the night. If he doesn't, I'm putting that on you," Munoz said furiously.

I didn't know what to do. So I decided, as ridiculous as it might sound, I needed to tell her the whole truth. I went back to the day I met Alex Reuben and everything that happened in Brazil. Then I told her about Anna and what I understood about the evil inside the men that had claimed her agents. Hearing the words come out of my own mouth, I knew she wouldn't buy it. I even had a hard time comprehending.

As my story came to a close, my fear had been confirmed. She looked at me like I belonged in an insane asylum, locked tightly in a strait jacket.

"Mr. Richards, how stupid do you think I am? Why would I believe something so ludicrous?"

What I said had just made things worse. Munoz opened the cell for a moment and punched me twice in the face before the others could pull her off of me.

Then she blurted out, in a completely unprofessional manner, "You're going to fry! You hear me?"

One of the men restraining her said, "Calm down, Munoz! The director wants to see you in his office right now!"

Reluctantly, she relaxed and walked back down the hallway. I was then sealed back in my cell.

Carla reached the FBI director's office, "Sir, you wanted to see me?"

"Yes, come in, have a seat."

Despite all the noise swirling around outside, his office was relatively quiet. He took his phone off the hook, closed the blinds surrounding the small room, and began to speak.

"With everything that occurred today, are you alright?"

"I'm fine, just some scrapes and bruises," Carla replied.

"I didn't mean physically alright," Director Williams continued.

"I'm scared for Darren."

He'd seemed satisfied with Carla's honest response. He settled himself in his chair and collected his thoughts. He knew what came next would be difficult for his prized agent, but professionally, it had to be done.

"I understand what you must be feeling, Munoz, but you can't just go flying off the handle. I don't have to tell you what beating a suspect in his cell looks like. Do you know what kind of heat that would bring down on this department if word got out? It's my recommendation, that in light of recent events with this case, you take a couple weeks off."

Carla instantly stood up, "Sir, are you asking me take a vacation?"

"No, I'm telling you that you are suspended with pay for two weeks. Effective immediately."

"What about the case?"

"Washington will be sending over some man power to fill the gap for those that were injured today."

Williams then stood up and walked over to Carla. She was visibly distraught, fury burning in her eyes. She was not one to back down.

He placed both hands on her shoulders and gave her a stern, authoritative look, "I've known you for years, and I consider you a friend as well as colleague. That's why I'm doing this for your own good. I don't want you anywhere near this case. It will be here when you get back, provided you don't pull anymore stunts like the one today."

"Yes, Sir," Carla said reluctantly.

She laid her badge and gun down on his desk, then sauntered out of the office.

Director Williams stopped her in the doorway, "The only thing you need to worry about right now is your partner. He could really use your support right now."

It took everything Carla had to suppress the unpleasant thoughts about her boss. She had deep respect for the man, but she felt his decision was out of line. Carla knew she was the best in her department and kicking her off the case was going to hinder any progress. She rolled her eyes and clenched her hands into fists before walking out of the office.

Back in the dreary cell, I questioned myself whether or not I should have told Munoz the truth. I nursed the wounds she had inflicted on my face. Clearly, it had been a mistake. I couldn't blame her though. I knew I sounded crazy. What was I suppose to do now? No one would believe me.

The agent assigned to watch me handed me some band aides and antiseptic wipes for the cuts on my face. I cleaned myself up the best I could and decided I should try to get some sleep. I would be in here for a while, no doubt. I was physically and emotionally drained. Little did I know, even sleep would not ease my restless mind.

The dream came again. I found myself lost to it as I had several times before.

Looking at my arms and hands, I could see I was wearing some type of armor. This was a new revelation, I hadn't noticed this in previous dreams. It began the same way it always did, complete chaos with people screaming and dying all around me. Others were running for their lives.

A woman cried out for me and I instantly felt sadness for her. I held her in my arms and every time, I watched her die. She told me, with her last breath, to take something and go to the light. Then, just like clockwork, I woke up.

This time, as I woke up, I began to draw a connection. I remembered the bones of the man in the ruins back in Brazil. He was wearing the same armor I had just seen in my dream. Was it possible that I was seeing the memories of this soldier? The very thought of it sent chills down my spine.

It was then that the director himself came to see me. He was unusually pleasant, given the fact he thought I was a mass murderer.

"How are you feeling?"

I shrugged my shoulders.

"I'd like to apologize for Agent Munoz's actions. I'll have someone bring you in something to eat. Then, we have a lot of questions for you."

"Okay," was all I wanted to say.

"Oh, and your wife is waiting outside. She doesn't know what happened in regards to your transport. Should I tell her to come over?"

"Yes, please," I wanted to cry.

"Enjoy your visit, it might be a long time until you see her again. And sorry, but we can't let her in there with you, you'll have to talk through the bars."

I nodded.

Sara walked in with her brave face on, but I knew inside, she was torn to bits. I knew it was more about me hiding things from her, not so much because of my incarceration.

"Are you okay, baby? What happened to your face?" she asked.

She reached through the bars and carefully touched the side of my bruised cheek.

"They roughed me up a little," I said, forcing a smile.

How could I have deceived this beautiful woman, my wife, for so long? It was for her own safety, I reminded myself. No matter how much our relationship had been strained, she was safe because of the lies I had told her.

Sara was a mess, but no matter what, she was always gorgeous to me.

"Did you come straight over in your pajamas?" I asked.

"Always the joker, just like your father, Eric," she was not amused.

My attempt to make light of the situation was to distract her from asking the deep questions. But, Sara knew me too well for that to work.

"You know Eric, you have some real explaining to do and you better start now. Our boys are at your mother's, scared, wondering if their father's coming home."

I looked at her and wanted more than anything, to tell her all of it. It hurt knowing I couldn't.

There was only one thing I could say, "I'm sorry honey, I just can't."

Sara went off and I didn't blame her, "Are you serious? After everything we've been through together!"

Her head sank, as though she honestly couldn't look at me.

Through clinched teeth and almost shaking lips from the anger, she asked me one more question, "Did you kill Robert and the rest of those people in Brazil?"

"No, I didn't. I'm surprised you would even ask that Sara!"

"Sorry hun, but what am I suppose to think? The way you've been acting lately, all secretive. You're sneaking out of the house and not telling me the truth about where you're going."

I never wanted any of this to happen. Since this whole thing had started, I was losing everything that was important to me. My father was the first. Now, my relationship with my wife was being threatened. I would soon lose my boys too. The worst part of it was not knowing what I was doing all this for. What was so important that it was worth sacrificing everything?

At that moment, I did the only thing I knew to do. Beyond the cold bars of the cell, I place both my hands on each side of Sara's face. I told her I was sorry for everything. Then I kissed her in the same way I had done the very first time on our third date.

"We'll get through this. I love you too much to ever let go of you," I promised her.

The man behind Sara looked at his watch and said, "Alright folks, five minutes, wrap this up."

"Promise me one more thing Eric. Promise me you'll come straight home when all of this gets sorted out," Sara said.

"Once they release me, we'll celebrate Christmas as a family, even if it's a little late."

Another man in a three piece suit walked in.

"You ready? It's time for your interrogation," he said dryly.

Sara told me again that she loved me and to call her when I was released.

As Sara walked away, the agent took me down the hallway to an even smaller room for questioning. There were two chairs and a table in the center of the room. On the table was a cup of coffee and a tape recorder. I knew the only way to get this over quickly was to devise a well-crafted lie. I was good at that, after all.

Apparently, the only witness to the murders was Alex Reuben. So, I told them I had left Brazil in a hurry because I found out two of Alex's men had murdered my father. I had feared for my own life. The truth was however, that I hadn't learned what had happened until the day after I returned home.

Calmly, I told the agent, who had been recording every word, "Question Alex Reuben and force him to give up those men, they're the real murderers. He's covering for them, using me as a scape-goat."

"We've had enough for now," the agent said.

He turned off the recorder and collected the papers in front of him.

"We had planned on bringing Mr. Reuben in for questioning on his claims. It won't be easy, given his high profile, but in the interest of both cases, it will be done. Photographs and his testimony alone won't be enough right now to charge you. Still, if we find any kind of proof that you are lying, this will go to trial. I suggest you get a lawyer just in case." He then motioned to the two-way mirror and the agent who had been watching me before, walked in and escorted me back to the isolated cell. I was left once again, with nothing but my own thoughts to dwell on. I was at the mercy of these men who knew nothing about me. Based on one man's accusation, they had made their own assumptions and I had instantly become a criminal. Things could not be any worse than this.

LESSONS

A s I was about to lose all hope, Anna suddenly appeared in front
of me. I was never so relieved to see someone in my entire
life. She traveled through the bars of my cell with a transpar-
ency that gave the impression she was a ghost in a dream. The
cell remained unscathed and the agents oblivious.

"Anna! You sure took your time finding me, could have used
your help a few hours ago," I was so happy to see her, I didn't
realize I was speaking too loud.

Before Anna could respond to my sarcasm, the man watching over me drew his pistol.

"Don't move," was all he said, not quite sure what to make
of the situation.

Anna instantly raised her hand in front of him. A surge of
white light burst from her dainty fingertips and the agent immediately fell to the floor, unconscious.

Anna saw the shock in my eyes and reassured me, "He's not
dead, but he will wake up with a severe headache and no memory
of you and me."

I didn't know why I was speechless. Considering all the events that had occurred in the last few weeks, nothing should surprise me anymore. I still had so many questions for Anna though. Like always, she sensed what I was thinking.

"There's no time for discussion, Eric, we need to leave now."

She held out her clenched fist to me, then opened it to reveal my father's necklace. It had been confiscated during my booking. I knew better than to ask how she recovered it.

"Put it on."

I complied and then she grasped my arm.

"Not again, I don't like traveling with you like this," I felt ill, globe hopping was rough on my equilibrium.

I focused on her crystal blue eyes to distract me from what was about to happen. The energy began to build, the same way it had in Brazil.

"Where are we going?" I asked.

"You'll see," she said, as the temperature of my body began to rise.

Seconds later, we had vanished from the building. Not a single shred of evidence was left in the cell.

Upon arrival at our destination, the first thing I noticed was we were knee deep in sand. The first thing that happened upon our arrival was me throwing up on that sand.

"I hate that," I said, taking deep breaths to steady my nerves.

"Before long, you'll get used to it," Anna chuckled.

"I don't want to get used to it. Has your kind ever heard of an airplane?"

She laughed even harder. It was nice she was taking such pleasure from my sickness. Despite the awful feeling in my stomach, I was alleviated to be out of that cell.

When the nausea finally passed, I raised my head to see the most beautiful temple. It was not like the one in Brazil. This temple was perfectly preserved. Surrounded by beautiful palm trees and lit up by the intense mid-day sun, the building was magnificent.

"Sara would love to see this," I muttered.

"Sorry Eric, we're not here to site see," Anna said, interrupting my bliss.

"You know, you have some real explaining to do about what happened in Philadelphia."

We walked into the massive structure. The ceiling stretched so high that I imagined it had taken years to construct. In fact, the whole building had probably taken decades to be completed. The temple had sprung up as an oasis in the middle of the dessert.

"I'm sorry, I thought there was a chance they'd be after you. I couldn't interfere though, you had to see how real the threat was for yourself," Anna finally said.

I grabbed her by the arm, "Wait just a minute, I could have been killed!"

She pulled away from my grip, "Not likely, Eric. Those two men were ordinary soldiers. Their powers were drastically less than Jason or Carter, and definitely less than Alex. I would have stepped in if I thought you couldn't handle them."

"But the truth is, I didn't do anything, Anna."

We walked to the center of the temple, where there was a large open space. In front of me was a large mural of some kind. Circling the open space were seven pillars, stretching to the ceiling. Half way up each pillar was a familiar writing, the same kind I had seen in the ruins in Brazil.

"Sure you did," Anna said with a large grin on her face.

Then she held out both her arms for dramatization and said, "This is it."

"Where are we?" I asked.

"Thirty-eight miles outside of Alexandria, Egypt. In this place, many of the faithful hid from persecution in order to keep their belief strong. Not long after that, this became a place of training for guardians, now more commonly called protectors."

"What's a protector?"

"You are! Some protectors are not called upon, but rather volunteer to become a protector.

You are unique, in that you share a direct bloodline to one of the seven chosen."

Anna continued to tell me of my part in some kind of great destiny. Then, she walked over to the mural and pushed in a circular emblem. It was made of stone, identical to the one around my neck. As she pushed the symbol, the ground began to shake and a large, square slab of rock in the roof retracted. Small amounts of sand streamed down from the opening in the ceiling. The sun shined through and illuminated the once dark center of the temple.

Anna opened up a large canvas bag she had brought with her. She pulled out some clothes and tossed them over to me.

"What's this for?" I asked.

"A change of clothes for you. I also have some tools you will need for training," She told me, eager to begin.

"I want to start right away. You are to listen to me and not question anything I am going to ask you to do. Are you ready?"

"I guess so," I said hesitantly.

We both changed into our new wardrobes, more suitable for the hot weather. Then, Anna took out some black sticks from her bag and tossed two of them to me.

"When we're done, you will no longer need to be afraid. We will stay here as long as it takes you to lose the fear and embrace the light of faith you have inside."

She instructed me to charge her and strike with the sticks she had given me. I ran straight at her, but within a split second, she moved and I fell to the floor.

As I spat sand out of my mouth, she tapped me on the back and said, "Again."

I stood and collected myself.

"Clear your mind this time. Focus on me. See past the obstacles of thought, and then strike me," Anna told me.

Every action and word echoed off the temple's cathedral-like ceiling.

"Also, remember to be mindful of your emotions. Do not let negative thoughts control you, or you won't even be able to make it beyond one encounter, Eric. Around your neck is a small connection to the very power of heaven. This should allow you to do many extraordinary things, as long as the faith and strength exists inside you."

"Really? That explains a few things," I was baffled.

"Don't get too excited, after all, you're still human. But, now you can heal very quickly from minor injuries. They can still kill you though, so keep your wits about you. Most importantly, remember that they can use your emotions, like anger, against you to make you turn on yourself or others you care about."

"Anna, I'll never be like them."

"Don't be over confident. They have turned many who have said the same thing. Now, back to training. Come at me again, but visualize it this time."

I stared at her for a moment, fully focused. I was completely unaware that necklace on my chest was beginning to glow again. I charged Anna again. This time, it was different. I moved with lightning speed. Everything else seemed to slow down and it was as though I could see her next move before she made it.

Anna jumped to the right as I passed her. But I turned around fast enough to strike her right leg before she landed on the ground.

"I'm so sorry! Did that hurt?" I was worried I had really injured her.

"No, not at all. It takes a lot for an angel to feel pain. Very good, Eric."

"Wow! That was amazing! What a rush!"

Anna was clearly amused by my reaction. She kept telling me 'again' and I successfully completed the task three more times. "Now, on to the basics of hand to hand combat."

Anna and I were so consumed by my training,

I hadn't even noticed that the writing on the pillars would glow white as we fought.

The lessons became more and more intense as the hours dragged on. When we stopped at the end of each day, Anna would leave and bring back food and water. It was only for me, angels had no need for food. Only her outer form was human.

The days turned into weeks, and yet for some reason, there seemed to be no concept of time in that place.

"Can we take a break?" I asked Anna, the intensity of the training was beginning to take a toll on my body.

"Sure," Anna was not winded at all.

I knew I looked terrible, given I had not showered or shaved during our entire stay at the temple. I collapsed to the ground and threw back another cup of water. Anna sat next to me and we began to talk.

"You've improved dramatically in the last few days, Eric," Anna observed.

"Does that mean we're almost finished here?" I was anxious to get home, concerned for Sara and the boys.

"Yes, almost," she replied.

Anna stared at me for a moment with her piercing blue eyes. I had learned that as she exerted her energy, her eyes would appear as a swirling pool of gold and white. She said nothing, leading me to believe she knew something.

"What is it?" I finally asked.

"The fate of the whole world rests in the hands of so few."

"What do you mean?"

Anna paused before answering, "I have been contemplating whether or not to tell you."

"Go on," I said impatiently.

"Right now, there are only a handful of boys and girls growing up, seven to be exact, who will one day know what you do. They will be the ones to either succeed or lose this war forever."

"What if they lose?"

"The whole world will plunge into darkness. The faithful will be killed and every other soul will be made into a mindless slave of evil. One of your own sons, Eric, will be the one to lead all the faithful followers."

Anna wouldn't tell me if the leader would be David or Michael. I did not like the idea at all and found the whole concept difficult to swallow. However, I knew it was useless to fight or deny the words of an angel. Anna said no one but her knew my son's role in this fight. I couldn't help but wonder if Alex Reuben or any other evil ones knew. If they didn't, someday the whole lot of them would.

"I didn't want to tell you at first. I was afraid you would try to protect them, just like your father did with you. Trust me Eric, it would not be good for you to know which of your sons will be the chosen."

Anna paused a moment before continuing, "There is one more thing I must tell you. Since this whole conflict began, the details and history of everything have been recorded in a special book. This book is thousands of years old and it grows with infinite pages every day. It includes information about the devil and his minions. It also contains the history of those who have bravely and selflessly given their lives for the greater good. This extraordinary collection is known as the 'Eternal Book' and one day, Eric, I hope you will write your own chapter in it as I have. I pray it is one of victory."

We sat silent for a few moments as I processed this bit of information.

"So what now?" I finally asked her.

"We continue with our lessons. We'll start with the blades. Then I will wound you with my own energy so you can teach yourself to heal."

For the first time during my training, I was a bit unnerved.

"Remember, you can heal from almost anything except a straight shot to the heart. Should your necklace be destroyed, that could kill you as well. This applies to the evil ones too. Only a bullet, blade, stake, or other implement to the heart will destroy them."

As soon as Anna was done speaking, without warning, she threw a blade past my shoulder and another directly into my stomach.

"Shit! Anna!"

"Focus, Eric. Pull out the blade and place your hand on the wound."

I did as she told me, "It hurts!"

My hand began to warm up and then glow white. It was the same glow my necklace produced. After a few minutes, the searing pain dissipated. I removed my hand and the wound was gone, only the blood remained.

Anna went on to tell me that once I was completely connected to the heavens, small wounds like the one I had just endured, would heal within seconds.

"If you suffer too many injuries at once, you will become physically drained. You will be weak, dizzy, and disoriented."

I was propped up next to one of the pillars, shocked by what had just happened. Anna sat down next to me and looked at where the puncture had been.

"Impressive," she whispered.

"What if things get really bad? Can you intervene?" I asked, hoping she would say yes to give me some comfort.

She took a deep breath, "Yes, but only in an extreme situation. There are rules, even if the dark ones have none, you and I do. I can only step in once. If I do, I am required to leave and never return."

I was too exhausted to ask why she would have to leave. It was evident my body was spent and I needed some rest.

"Are we done, Anna?"

"I must show you how to block bullets, something you can only do if you anticipate them coming. You should eat something first, then sleep for a bit. You need to regain your strength."

I quickly faded away and fell into a deep sleep, dreaming of my family. Michael and David were in the back yard with my mom, building a snow man, while Sara looked on from the kitchen window. The smell of her famous apple pie permeated the crisp winter air. Smooth jazz filled the living room as I relaxed in a chair next to the fireplace, intently reading the morning paper. This must be what heaven looks like.

Anna woke me up, frantically telling me we had to finish my training. It seemed like only a few moments I had been asleep, but I knew it was more like a few hours. I ate a couple bites of bread and took a sip of water before telling her I was ready.

"Go to the other side of the room."

I once again did as I was told. I could sense I was about to be impaled again. Sure enough, Anna pulled a pistol out of her bag of weapons.

"Put at least one hand up," she instructed.

I hesitantly raised my right hand in front of me. Anna fired the gun. Just as the bullet arrived to me on the other side of the room, I saw my eyes begin to glow white and gold in the reflection of the rotating lead. It was in the same manner as Anna's eyes had been. At the same time, strange words came into my mind and out my mouth. It was a language I had heard before, but did not understand.

"Et arlon vedoska a lon."

The bullet ricocheted off an almost invisible shield in front of my hand.

"What was that?" I asked, the shield diminishing and my eyes returning to normal.

"You said, 'Where His light never fades'. It's scripture. You are speaking the language of heaven, the same language that is written on these pillars."

"That was amazing, Anna!" I said, still stunned from what had just happened.

"You're ready, Eric. My job here is done. I believe you are well prepared and it's time for you to return home."

Was it safe for me to go home? Wouldn't the police be looking for me?

Once again, Anna knew what I was thinking, "Yes, they will be looking for you. There is one rule you must never break, under any circumstance. You must never kill innocent people."

She packed up our gear as I reflected on our time in the temple. The training had been grueling and I wanted to give up so many times. I never gave Anna any indication of that though. She had a mission to prepare me for a fight and I had a mission not to disappoint her. We had both persevered and now that we were at the end, I felt a great sense of accomplishment.

"We are going back for the artifact, Eric. Your wife should be working, giving us plenty of time to acquire it."

I knew Sara must have been worried sick, not knowing what had happened to me or where I had been for nearly three weeks. How could I explain my vanishing from the cell at the police station? I knew by all means, I had to keep her out of this.

"Shall we get going?" Anna asked.

I couldn't imagine any other place I wanted to be than home in Philadelphia.

Anna and I locked hands as we had done several times before.

The amount of energy that build up before the transport never ceased to amaze me. However, nothing could have prepared me for what had been planned for my arrival on the other side.

Rise Against

The next thing I knew, I was laying in the creek behind my house. Anna was the unfortunate one this time and ended up in the snow. My body was in shock, going from extreme heat to extreme cold. I was soaking wet, wearing nothing but shorts and a tank top. Anna rushed over and pulled me out of the water, then we sprinted into the house.

As expected, no one was home. I did my best not to leave evidence of me being in the house. I bolted up the stairs intent on a hot shower. I stopped only for a moment at the top of the stairs when 'February' on the calendar caught my eye. Was it really February? Anna and I had been gone only three weeks, and yet back in the real world, it had been two months. My need to raise my body temperature overtook my curiosity so I quickly hopped into the shower.

Drying myself off, I examined my haggard appearance in the mirror. The stress from recent events had not been kind to me. I was pulling a fleece sweatshirt over my head when Anna knocked on the door.

"Eric, I can't stay long," she said.

"Where are you going?" I asked, confused.

"There is someone else I need to go see."

Of course she was as cryptic as ever and refused to say who it was or explain why.

"You need to get the artifact and take it where no one will see you," Anna continued.

"Okay, then what?"

"That piece around your neck is also a key. You will know where to go once you've used it."

Before I could say another word, Anna transported out of the house. Following her directions, I went into the bedroom and opened my safe. I took out the metallic block, still confused by the mystic powers it supposedly possessed. I grabbed my green backpack out of the closet and carefully placed the cube inside, wrapping it in some spare clothes.

I slung the bag over my shoulder and went downstairs to gather some food for the road. I wasn't sure where I was going or how long I would be gone. I looked out the kitchen window and saw that Sara had taken my jeep to work, leaving me with my motorcycle as the only option. It was a little too frigid outside for two wheels but at least the roads were clear. I put on an extra jacket and a pair of gloves and headed for the garage.

I knew exactly where I would stow the artifact. The new office my company was due to move into in the springtime sat isolated and abandoned on the other side of town.

The roar of my eight-two Ducati brought back memories of long summer rides. It had been a gift from another project my company had handled. The private investor was extremely grateful for our findings and very generous in his gratuity.

It was nearly six o'clock, the sun had set and Sara would be home soon. I looked back at the house one more time, holding back the lump that was forming in my throat, then pulled out onto the street. Immediately after I left the garage, I had the distinct feeling I was being watched. I subtly scanned the area and saw someone in a tan car down the opposite side of the street watching me intently. As I passed the car, I looked the man directly in the eyes, it was Carter, no doubt.

I wasn't sure how he had found me so fast. Anna and I had only arrived less than an hour ago. I didn't have time to linger on the thought, so I gunned the bike, hoping I could out-run him. I weaved in and out of traffic and watched as Carter struggled to keep up. Then I noticed another car racing up behind Carter. It was a black van, with what looked like cops inside.

Inside the van sat several men in white shirts and ties from the FBI. They'd been staking out the Richards' home, day and night for weeks, hoping Eric would return.

In the tan car, the men began shouting at each other.

"Carter, get closer!" yelled Jason.

Moving dangerously fast, they sped through red lights and stop signs, leaving a trail of wrecked cars behind them.

I narrowly escaped the traffic slamming into each other. We were now racing down the freeway. The tan car was gaining on me. It pulled up beside me as Jason rolled down the passenger's side window, revealing an automatic weapon. He began firing on me. I ducked and began swerving back and forth to avoid the shots.

The black van was still in site and began speeding up to the car. Slamming into the rear of Carter and Jason's vehicle, you could hear the sound of breaking taillights as the van hit.

Carter yelled at Jason, "Take care of them now!"

Jason climbed into the back seat and busted out the back window with one swift punch from his fist. Pointing his gun out the open window, he began firing straight into the grill and windshield of the van. The van immediately swerved in response into the opposite lane, running straight into an oncoming pickup truck. Both vehicles stopped dead in their tracks while Carter and Jason continued their pursuit.

I reached into my jacket and took out the pistol Anna had given me. I started shooting at the car, hitting Carter several times, which slowed them down only a little. I took the exit that would lead me to the office building and frantically tried to slow down, as I realized I was still going in excess of seventy miles per hour. Before I knew it, I found myself sliding sideways on the pavement, the street tearing up my jeans right down to my skin.

I came to a stop in the middle of a four way intersection. I laid there for a moment, as all the cars surrounding me stopped at the site of me crashing such a beautiful bike. There was no time to pick it back up.

I dusted myself off and used my healing abilities to close the open wounds I had suffered. Looking behind me, I could see headlights from the tan car careening through the other vehicles, popping off side mirrors. I was boxed in by the curious bystanders, who had abandoned their cars in the intersection. Carter and Jason were nearly on top of me.

I thought on pure instinct of survival and shouted, "Not today!"

The energy built quickly within my arms, glowing an extremely bright white. It discharged with such a kick, that my entire body shifted back nearly four feet. Carter had come within inches of hitting me. The combined force of their speed and the impact of my energy caused the tan car to launch sideways. It violently traveled to the left and slammed into the front of two other vehicles that were stopped in the intersection.

I paused only for a second in shock of how I was able to toss the car as if it were a toy. All I could do from there was run. I was fortunate in that I was only a few blocks from the uninhabited office building. I had bought myself just enough time to get away.

In a frenzy, I ran down the sidewalks, pushing people aside. I continued to look behind my shoulder, expecting to see Carter and Jason chasing me at any second. Random thoughts entered and exited my mind as I maneuvered through pedestrians. I knew there was no way I could fight off one of them, let alone both. I wasn't strong enough, not yet anyway.

I was breathing heavily and desperately tried to catch my breath. I was relieved when I finally saw the building across the street. Our future office was located on the fifth floor. I wasn't sure if the plan was still in motion. Without me, Cove Corporation was leaderless, and without my relentless crew, only secretaries and assistants remained. The thought of my men being executed only made me run faster.

Upon reaching the building, I took the back end of my pistol and broke out the first floor entrance windows. After carefully stepping through the now open sliding doors, I raced up the several flights of stairs to the fifth floor. I was right, the entire building sat empty.

I reached my destination and found a table to set my backpack on. I chugged the bottle of water I had packed as I reached for the artifact.

"This is it," I said to myself.

I carefully removed the cube from the cloth it had been wrapped in and placed it on the floor.

"Now what?" as if I was expecting it to answer me.

The object could hardly be seen within the walls of the dark room. I sat down on the floor in front of it and began to have my doubts. Surely, this had not been a colossal waste of time. My frustration was beginning to get the best of me. Looking around the destitute office, I realized my crew, my friends, had died for this piece of trash.

I stood up and kicked the object across the room. Just as it slid to a stop, the artifact began to shake. It then leaped up into the air, eye level with me, and hovered still. I walked closer towards it and as I did, the medallion around my neck lifted up slowly to meet the cube. It was as though the two objects were magnets. The stone in the center of my necklace began to shine like a Roman candle, nudging me ever so close to the levitating artifact.

"What the...my God, it's so...," I couldn't speak.

The writing along the sides of the cube were now visible enough to read. Somehow, this magnificent power enabled me to comprehend it.

It read, "They were hand-picked by His gracious and most powerful right hand. Seven chosen to guide those lost in darkness. With the light of His most perfect love, they shall fight the pestilence with clean hands and pure hearts. Until the day of our Lord's arrival, will they ever be tried and tested, of which their faith may prove able and unwavering."

I couldn't move or even feel my own body, as if I was paralyzed. Oddly enough, I was not afraid. My feet began to lift off the ground as my head aligned with the metallic cube. A beam of light originating from the cube then shined directly into my eyes. I was completely powerless, unable to react. I began to see images of different places and random information. Every second, a barrage of information was forced into my mind at such an intense rate, it became unbearably painful.

I finally couldn't tolerate it anymore and began to scream. My necklace that had been hovering in front of me, launched backwards and struck me in the face. At the same time, the metal artifact dropped to the ground, as did I.

I laid there on the floor, in the middle of the empty office, for what seemed like an eternity. I only began to come to when I felt familiar hands on my shoulders, shaking me awake. I could feel the warmth of blood streaming from my nose and ears. The shaking of my shoulders was relentless, I knew very well those soft hands. I forced my eyes open.

"Sara?" I thought for sure I was hallucinating.

"I'm sorry, Eric, they made me. Please tell me what's going on," my wife said, confusion engulfing her eyes.

That's when I noticed Carter and Jason standing behind Sara, guns aimed at her back. I could see bruises on her wrists, as if she had been tied up as a prisoner. Her eyes were red and dried tears still adhered to her beautiful face. She was scared, looking to her husband for answers.

"You're not looking too good, Eric. Nice move flipping our car back there. Not too smart with your wife in the backseat though," Jason laughed.

Sarah was about to speak again when Carter covered her mouth with duct tape. Jason quickly bound her wrists behind her back.

"Sara!" I protested.

"Shut up!" Jason ordered and kicked me in the ribs three times.

"Enough, Jason!" Carter snapped

Sara was then thrown on the floor a few feet away from me.

"You know why we're here, don't you?" Carter continued.

"Take it! Just leave my wife alone!" I cried hysterically.

Jason found the cube lying on the floor next to the window and picked it up, "At last, victory is ours. It's time to reveal our true selves and rule this land!"

Carter was now holding a gun to my head, Sara looked on helplessly.

"What are you waiting for? Destroy it!" Carter shouted.

Jason positioned his hands on each side of the artifact. As he did, a small amount of energy seemed to splinter through the cube, shattering the artifact into dozens of pieces. Sara looked at me absolutely terrified. All I wanted to do was hold her.

"Let's see their prophecy come to pass now," Jason commented.

"What are you going to do to us?" I asked, assuming they would kill us both.

Jason asked Carter the same thing, to which Carter replied, "There's no need to do anything, since no one in their right mind would ever believe them. Besides, we destroyed the cube. Without it, the final piece that posed any threat to us, is gone. It's time to inform the master of our great triumph, he will be quite pleased."

Carter lowered his gun as Jason walked over to me, stepping on the shards of metal, and kicked my ribs once again.

"Consider yourself very lucky, you piece of shit. You better hope this is the last time we see each other. I would love nothing more than to kill you slowly," Jason said in his sinister tone.

Both men then walked silently out of the room, leaving Sara and I lying on the floor. With only the streetlights outside illuminating the dark room, I crawled across the floor to Sara. I tore the tape off her mouth and untied the rope around her wrists. She immediately fell into my arms and I held her tightly.

"It's going to be alright, honey. I'm so sorry, I had no idea you were in the backseat of that car. Are you alright?" I pleaded.

"I'm okay, just some scrapes and bruises. Eric, what's going on?"

Then she placed both hands on my face, examining the dried blood from my ears and nose. She kissed me lightly on the forehead and insisted on looking at my side where Jason had repeatedly kicked me.

"We need to get you to a hospital," Sara finally said.

"No, I'm fine. How would I explain this anyways?"

I realized in that moment, that it was time for Sara to know everything. I could no longer hide anything from this amazing woman. We helped each other off the floor and began making our way out of the building. Once we had made it to the street below, I began to explain all that had happened, beginning with the necklace Dad had left me. I was surprised at how receptive she was.

"Where are the kids?" I asked.

"They're still at your mother's. I was on my way to pick them up and they grabbed me before I reached the front door," Sara replied.

We walked slowly, hand in hand, down the sidewalk. I would never again let her go.

"Eric, I've always known that God had a destiny for you. He has a plan for all of us. But this, this is a lot to digest."

I looked over at her, overwhelmed myself, and nodded.

"What do we do now? Is it really over? Won't the whole world be plunged into darkness?" She asked, waiving down an approaching taxi.

Sara had too many questions and I didn't have enough answers, so I did the best I could. Where was Anna when I needed her?

Distant Lands

We stepped into the cab as the driver asked where we would like to go. Sara gave him the address for my mother's house. As the cab pulled out onto the street, I began to tell Sara why she had been taken and why Jason and Carter destroyed that cube.

"The artifact was destroyed, but before it was, it loaded something into my brain. I think part of it was the location of where I'm suppose to go next."

"I'm going with you. Like it or not, I'm involved now and I'm not leaving you again," Sara said firmly, leaving no room for discussion.

She could tell by the expression on my face I was not pleased with the idea. Being the stubborn woman I love, I knew there was no use in arguing with her.

"What about the boys?" was all I said.

"We could take them to my brother Arthur's house in New York, they should be safe there.

"You know Sara, once they figure out what happened, that I have the information from the cube, they'll come after us."

"I know," she said.

The taxi stopped in front of Mom's house.

Sara paid the driver and we both prepared ourselves for an interrogation. My mother was worried sick when Sara never showed to pick the kids up. Lucky for us, she had hadn't reached the brink of calling the cops yet, we had come home just in time.

"What happened to you two?" was her first question, as expected.

"Car accident. Don't worry, we're fine," I told her, it was best to lie.

Michael and David ran into the foyer at the sound of our voices. Sara and I each knelt down and hugged them tightly, doing our best to suppress our tears. The boys told me how much they missed me since the bad policemen had taken me away.

"Eric, let's get you cleaned up."

"Yes, mother," I said in a sarcastic but loving tone.

"Boys, Daddy's not feeling well. Go play in the living room, he'll be down in a little bit," Mom told David and Michael.

The boys reluctantly obliged and Mom took me to the upstairs bathroom to tend to my wounds. It broke my heart to think about the boys becoming orphans if something were to happen to Sara and myself. I took some comfort in knowing that one of them was a chosen leader.

My mother did an exceptional job of treating my injuries. She made me take my shirt off to better see the bruises on my ribs. Then she noticed the medallion around my neck.

"I've seen that before," she said, as though it brought back memories.

"It was Dad's, he left it for me," I told her.

She accepted my answer and seemed to drop the subject. I could tell that talking about Dad was still a sensitive topic. She took a washcloth and cleaned up my bruises, then wrapped a bandage around my ribcage. I knew I could use the necklace to heal myself, but this was not the time, nor the place.

"I think you're good to go, son. Tell Sara to come up so I can look at her too," Mom said.

"Of course, thanks Mom," I replied with a smile, giving her a kiss on the cheek.

Two FBI agents walked into the emergency room at St. Mary's Hospital, fully intent on questioning the only surviving agent from the ambushed convoy. He'd been in critical condition for weeks, and lucky to be alive.

The wounded agent struggled through the pain to explain the events that had landed him in the hospital. He had suffered broken ribs, a collapsed lung, internal bleeding, and many severe lacerations all over his body. The two men listened attentively, occasionally jotting down notes in their booklets.

As the FBI was wrapping up their questioning of the fallen agent, Carla Munoz burst through the door, searching for the survivor herself. Sadness filled her eyes, remembering the loss of Darren just months before.

"What are you doing here?" she asked the agents.

"Agent Munoz, if you don't mind, I think you should turn around and walk out of here," one of the agents said firmly.

"Excuse me?" Carla was not respectable towards the agency for their involvement in her last case.

"This is not your case anymore."

"Since when?"

"Since your only suspect in this case escaped custody. Not only was he suspected of mass murdering his entire crew, but it happened in Brazil, making this an international situation as well."

"His men killed my partner!" Carla was becoming ever more irate.

"We are aware of that and very sorry. We will get to the bottom of this, but you need to let us do our job."

Just then, the young man lost his battle for life. The doctor and nurses responded quickly to the sound of the flat line. They scrambled to resuscitate the man, but it was too late. The doctor called time of death as one of the nurses pulled the sheet over his lifeless body. Carla left the room without saying another word, distraught and angry.

The agents walked out into the hallway where they began to discuss their next move.

"Make sure Ms. Munoz doesn't interfere with this investigation another second," the senior agent advised his partner.

The man obliged his superior and immediately got on the phone with Carla's supervisor. She was terminated from the agency the following morning.

Sipping instant coffee from the hospital vending machine, the senior agent said, "Mr. Richards was spotted at his home today by one of our agents. Once again, somehow he escaped being detained. We start there."

Carter and Jason arrived at the back entrance of a metal recycling plant, followed by four other men dressed in black.

"Where's Alex?" Jason grumbled.

Just then, Alex Reuben emerged from the shadows, giving Jason a menacing look. The men gathered around their leader as he began to speak.

"I have asked you all here for two reasons," Alex began.

Before he could continue, a man from the plant's security walked up on the meeting.

"You can't be here, you're trespassing!" the security guard shouted.

"Let me at him," Jason muttered with a smirk.

"You, show me your hands slowly," the man said, pointing at Alex.

"Certainly, anything you say," Alex responded sarcastically.

As Alex raised his hands, the molten metal in the vat next to the guard began to transform into a pillar, reaching high into the air. When Alex was satisfied with what he had created, he abruptly dropped his hands. The liquid metal dropped as well, falling on top of the guard, covering him from head to toe. The guard screamed and shouted in agony before collapsing to the ground.

"Where were we?" Alex asked, collecting his thoughts.

"Sir, we destroyed the artifact," Carter said with great pride.

"Good. Now, I need you gentlemen to get the boy. It's time we prepared for the master's arrival. He wants the boy trained immediately."

"What boy?" Jason asked.

"The one called David, Eric Richards' son. The master wants him for the transfer."

"Yes, Sir," the men said in unison.

Then Alex looked over at Carter and seemed to be very displeased.

"Did you and Jason check the artifact to see if it had been used before you destroyed it?" he asked.

A look of dread came over Carter, "No, but when we arrived, we found Eric laying on the floor."

Alex ordered all the men accept Carter to go and retrieve the boy. No one, including Jason, had ever seen Carter so afraid. He had turned white as a sheet, paralyzed with fear.

When they were alone, Alex addressed Carter, "Was Eric bleeding from his ears and nose?"

"Yes, how did you know that?" Carter was confused.

Alex grabbed him tightly by the arms, "Because I killed a girl many, many years ago, who had activated the piece, she showed the same symptoms. Then she'd handed it off to another man who hid the same artifact in Brazil."

Alex was growing more agitated as Carter began to fear for his life.

"You idiot, Carter. Everything that was in that piece is now in Eric's head. You'd better kill him before he figures out what it means."

Then, Alex looked deep into Carter's eyes and said, "I gave you this vessel and I can take it away if you fail me again."

Carter was violently tossed to the ground as Alex said one last thing, "Get out of my site, you have a job to do."

Carter dusted himself off, still reeling from Alex's threat. He joined the rest of the men waiting outside the gate, doing his best not to show his trembles.

At my mom's house, we were all sitting down to a lovely family dinner. She had been hard at work in the kitchen, insisting that a hearty meal was just what Sara and I needed. David and Michael sat opposite from us, while Mom sat at the head of the table. There was an obvious empty chair at the other end. I paused and stared briefly, our family would never be the same again.

Mom broke the silence with a comment about our car accident, "Did you get that man's insurance info who hit you?"

"Yes Mother, of course," I said quickly, signifying my desire to change the subject.

The fire burned bright in the living room, adding to the coziness throughout the house. Despite the blazing fire, we were still bundled up in an array of sweaters. The spread of food was absolutely wonderful, almost as if it were the Christmas dinner we had missed together. Over the years, what we had enjoyed most about Mom's cooking, was the sheer variety she would bring to the table.

For the first time in months, every stress and worry seemed to vanish as life was normal once again. Sara and I reveled in the moment, which was sure to pass all too soon.

We both knew it.

My wife was the first one to excuse herself from the table. She escorted the boys upstairs and did her best not to show the stresses that gripped her heart.

"I'm going to tuck the boys in and read them a story," she said.

Before she left, I whispered in her ear, "We need to talk when you come back."

I didn't want to give Mom any indication of the issues we were having. I wouldn't know where to begin if she began to ask questions. I went back to the table and helped clear the dishes and put the leftovers in the fridge.

"Hey Mom, I'll take care of those dishes. You just relax," I told her, taking a dish out of her hands as she made her way to the sink.

"Thank you, son. I'm so proud of the man you have become. I don't care what anybody else says, you're a good man," she replied.

Before my hands reached the soapy dish water, I began to question everything, mainly the safety of my family. Then I wondered what would be lost at the hands of those minions of evil if Sara and I failed the purpose designed for us. I imagined a world like Anna described, nothing but evil and darkness. The whole planet would be filled with nothing more than mindless zombies, innocent civilians possessed by demonic powers. The army of lifeless darkness would be intent on only one thing, the destruction of all that is good and just. Heaven itself, would be destroyed.

How could I, being only one man, make any kind of impact against such a threat to humanity? Before I could let my thoughts wander any further, Sara came down the stairs for our talk.

"You had something you wanted to talk about, dear?" she asked.

"Yes, let's go to the guest room. Mom doesn't need to hear this," I said as she kissed me on the cheek.

We went into the bedroom and made sure the door was secured behind us. Sara sat on the bed in front of me, waiting for me to talk first.

"You're right, we need to take the boys to your brother's place. I don't know what to tell him when we just drop them off without notice, but we don't have any other options," I said.

"I know," was all she said.

Then I sat on the bed next to her and held her in a loving embrace. I reassured Sara everything would be okay once the kids were safe. I had to reassure myself too.

"Babe, do you think we could stop by Dad's grave before we leave? I think I will be able to make sense of all those images I saw if I was close to my father again. Maybe I can figure out what the next step will be."

"Of course, honey," Sara replied.

The next morning, Sara and I prepared the boys as if they were on their way to school. We thought it was best not to tell them where they were going. It was eight o'clock when we said good-bye to my mother. I told her I loved her and gave her a kiss on the forehead. Then we headed out towards the cemetery.

Sara waited in the jeep with David and Michael while I went to talk to Dad.

"I wish you were here, more than anything, Dad. Everything was so much clearer when you were around, you had an answer for everything. I don't know if I can handle the things Anna said would be coming in my future. I need your strength."

I looked back at Sara as if to let her know I was almost done. I had one more thing to tell the late and great Fredric Richards.

"I promise I will get the men who killed you, if it's the last thing I ever do."

As if a sign from the heavens, it began to downpour. I pulled my hood over my head and ran back to the Jeep.

Sara placed her hand on mine as I glanced back at the twins, who were fast asleep.

"They must have been playing last night instead of sleeping," Sara commented with a smile.

Not too far from the cemetery, Samantha Richards' house was being closely inspected by Carter and Jason. They sat in their car across the street, looking for any signs of life.

"They're not here. Can you find them?" Jason asked, looking out the side window.

Carter immediately turned the car off and began to focus. He stared straight ahead, his eyes began to haze over. Within his mind, he saw every location Eric and Sara had been, with a bird's eye view on their Jeep going down the highway. He turned his head to see the sign on the freeway as if he were standing next to it.

"What do you see?" Jason inquired anxiously.

"They're taking the freeway exit to New York," Carter said.

"Let's go!" Jason shouted, interrupting Carter's concentration.

Carter's eyes returned to normal, "Don't ever distract me when I'm phasing."

Carter had made up the word 'phasing' to describe his ability. He was the only one of their kind who could phase that far out.

"What about Fredric's wife?" Jason asked.

"She's a clueless, feeble old woman. We have no need to kill her."

"But we could at least ask."

"No, Jason. If she saw our faces, we would have to kill her. I'm not going to eliminate anyone unless it's to our benefit."

Jason began to think Carter was losing his edge.

Killing was what they did best.

My brother-in-law, Arthur, was as distant as any family member could be. He had gone through a fallout with their dad over a trivial matter, I couldn't even remember what it was. Their relationship had been so strained, at his funeral, Arthur was nowhere to be seen. Sara had always wondered if their issues stemmed from Arthur being adopted.

Sara, having such a kind heart, learned to forgive her brother. She loved him as though he were blood, even though they hadn't spoken in years. The silence between them made the decision to leave the kids with him that much more difficult. However, our family was small and we didn't have any other options.

We arrived at Arthur's house a little hesitant. He lived in a decent suburban neighborhood, north of New York City.

Sara knocked on the door. With no answer, she walked around to the backyard and found her brother with a poll saw, trimming his overgrown bushes.

I collected our boys and followed Sara to the side of the house. I barely recognized Arthur. A year had passed since he had lost his wife to cancer. Apparently, he wasn't coping well. I couldn't blame him.

"Sara!" he said, rushing over to give his sister a hug.

"Arthur, I've missed you so much," Sara said.

I walked into the yard with David and Michael holding each of my hands. This man was practically a stranger to the twins.

"Eric, good to see you. Wow, the boys are getting so big!"

I shook Arthur's hand and introduced him to the boys. As expected, David and Michael didn't remember him at all. Although slightly weary, they seemed excited at the thought of their long lost uncle.

"Let's all go inside and warm up," Arthur suggested with enthusiasm.

This man had clearly been an outcast for far too long. Under different circumstances, I would have loved to enjoy this family reunion. However, Sara and I had very little time before we were discovered. This was about protecting the boys, not reminiscing about the past.

"Cup of coffee?" Arthur asked Sara and I from the kitchen.

"No thanks, we can't stay long," I replied.

Sara took the boys into the living room where they found the TV and immediately turned on the cartoon tapes they had brought with them.

"It's really great to see you guys, I don't know where the time went. The twins were learning to crawl the last time I saw them," Arthur observed.

I smiled and nodded, not knowing how to respond. Then Sara walked in to the kitchen and interrupted the awkward silence.

There was no easy way to ask such a favor, so Sara got straight to the point, "Arthur, I know its short notice, but would you watch the boys for a few days?"

"What's wrong, are you in some kind of trouble?" Arthur's demeanor instantly changed.

"No," I said a little too fast.

"Eric and I just need some time to ourselves to take care of few things. Samantha needs a break too. Just a few days, that's all. They're easy to watch, well behaved, and excited to get to know their uncle," Sara explained.

Arthur knew from the look on Sara's face that she wasn't being completely honest with him. Thankfully the love he had for his sister abolished his suspicions and he reluctantly agreed.

"Sure, of course I will. They'll be a good distraction. Everything will be fine," Arthur was convincing himself more than us.

After some more small talk and a few instructions regarding the boys, Sara and I returned to the living room. The boys were fully engrossed in their show until Sara turned it off and insisted on a hug from both of them.

"You're going to stay here with Uncle Arthur for a while. I want you to be on your best behavior and listen to what he says. Your father and I will be back in a few days. I love you both so much."

I hugged the boys after Sara finally let them go and told them I loved them too. I could tell they were confused and distraught over their parents leaving them with a stranger. It took everything I had to keep the tears that were welling up from spilling over.

When we finally made it back to the Jeep, I could see Sara was already crying silently.

"There's a chance we might not be back, isn't there?" she asked me.

With that, she broke down, sobbing hysterically. I pushed aside the hair from her cheek and wiped the tears from her beautiful face. There was nothing I could say that would ease her concerns. I knew the reality of the situation, just like she did.

Fifteen minutes later, Sara and I were back on the road, in search of a library. We had no idea how long it was going to take in finding the place we both needed to go. Sara had a brilliant idea that would hopefully help and the first step was finding a library.

We proceeded down the street until we came upon a phone booth. Sara got out and rifled through the phone book until she found the address of a local library. Jumping back into the car, she took the map out of the glove compartment and began to navigate.

Whenever Sara got something in her head, she had an extremely focused look in her eyes. I called it 'the zone'. Once she was in the zone, there was no use in asking her anything. When she was ready to talk, she would tell you. I had never seen her so angry and sad at the same time, two emotions that seemed to fuel her mission.

The library was small, but still sufficient enough that Sara was confident she would find what she was after. As for me, I had no idea what was circulating through that half-crazed brain of hers. She asked the librarian for some blank paper and then told me to take a seat. I had complete faith in this woman, so I did as I was told and let her do her thing.

Just a few minutes later, she returned to the table with an armful of books.

"Now, are you going to tell me what you're doing?" I asked her.

"We are in this together, Eric. Like you said, there's not a lot of time before they catch up to us."

Sara opened one of the books and looked at me like I knew what I was suppose to do.

She continued, "I believe this will work. I want you to close your eyes and dig deep to find those images you saw before. Describe what you see and I will draw it out on paper. Then, I should be able to find them in these geography books."

"That's brilliant, Sara!" I was thoroughly impressed by her quick thinking.

Sara then picked up a pencil and waited anxiously over a piece of paper. Seeing she was ready, I closed my eyes and concentrated on that moment when the artifact blasted my mind.

At first, there was nothing but the back of my eye lids to stare at.

"This isn't working," I told Sara, annoyed.

Before she could respond, a myriad of images flooded my head.

"There's too many, too fast."

"Can you slow them down and focus on one?" Sara asked.

That was the last thing I remember Sara saying. I'm not sure when, but at some point, I went into a trance-like state. I was completely oblivious to what I had been saying in the hour that had passed. According to Sara, I had been describing roads and tunnels and some kind of cathedral.

Sara began to worry and snapped me out of the trance with a swift slap to side of my face. Others in the library, interrupted by the commotion, looked at us slightly disturbed. I was dazed and disoriented. I kept fading in and out for a few minutes before finally returning to reality.

"What happened? Did it work?" I asked, my vision still foggy.

"Yes Eric, it worked. I've never seen you like that before, it was a little upsetting. Your eyes were open and you were looking around, but you weren't really here."

"I know, it was like I was really there. I could feel, hear and even smell everything."

I finally looked down at the table where several sketches were scattered about. Sara had done a splendid job of drawing my images. Wasting no time, we each grabbed a book and began searching for anything that may have been a match.

Once again, the whole room looked at us when Sara exclaimed, "That's got to be the place!"

She handed the book over to me, pointing at one of the pictures. It was one of the most famous cathedrals in the middle of Paris. I looked back at Sara's drawing, then to the book several times, before confirming it was one in the same. It was certainly a match, from the street to the church itself. It was Notre Dame Cathedral.

We left the United States that night from JFK Airport, on our way to France. My wife and I were literally and figuratively, taking this journey in the dark. We knew our destination, but we had no clue what we would find when we got there, nor did we know what we were looking for.

Sara was an uneasy passenger, she never liked to fly. She spent the first two hours of the long flight squeezing my left hand, leaving an imprint from my wedding band that lasted for a week. I did my best to calm her worries and she eventually fell asleep on my shoulder. As I watched her sleep, I realized there was no way in hell I could have come this far without her. She was a truly amazing woman and I happened to be married to her.

I began to doze off myself as the pilot announced we were four hours away from Paris. As I closed my eyes, I had no idea that another pair of eyes were watching my every move.

These threatening eyes belonged to Jason, who was eagerly awaiting an opportunity to kill us.

All was quiet in the little New York suburb at Arthur's house. The stillness didn't last long as Carter pulled up across the street from the house. David and Michael were playing baseball in the yard, unattended by any adults.

Carter, along with another follower, seized the opportunity and jumped out of the car. Carter snatched up David while the other man grabbed Michael to stifle his screams. Quickly, Carter wrestled the boy into the car.

Once David was secured in the vehicle, Carter yelled to the other man, "Let's go!"

As soon as he was released, Michael ran full speed to his uncle's house screaming, "They took David!"

Everything unfolded in just seconds and the neighborhood remained unaware of the abducted boy.

On the other side of the world, Sara and I arrived at Paris International Airport.

"I felt something really strange on the plane, Sara. It was the same feeling I had when I was being transported to jail, before the convoy incident. Only, this was much stronger."

"What do you think it was, babe?"

Sara asked as we made our way out of the terminal.

"I don't know, but we have more important things to worry about now," I replied, doing my best to shake the uneasy feeling.

We wasted little time in hailing a taxi to the nearest hotel. Paris was absolutely beautiful, beyond words. I had only seen the city in movies, which hardly did the place justice. Everywhere, the streets were packed with pedestrians, making their way through the vendors and buskers. If only we could have experienced the sites outside of the taxi.

"Now Eric, why didn't we come here for our honeymoon?" Sara asked, jabbing me in the shoulder with her fist.

I had to suppress my laugh, "Because I was broke with barely two pennies to rub together."

She smiled, then laughed, "I remember how much my father protested me marrying you because you weren't much better off than he was."

I thought back to that moment when Sara's father sat me down and asked how I expected to give her all the things his little princess deserved. I'd say my response was good enough to win any father's blessing.

In faith, I told him, "Sir, she won't lack anything as long as she lives, I promise."

Back in New York, Carter arrived at Alex Reuben's building with David Richards.

"You will behave when we see Mr. Reuben," Carter told David in the elevator.

Seventy floors up the skyscraper sat Reuben's office.

"Go right in, gentlemen. Mr. Reuben is expecting you," the receptionist announced upon their arrival.

Carter practically dragged the boy in by the arm.

"Ah, yes, David Richards, we've been waiting for you for some time now," Alex said, standing in front of the massive window.

"We've got big plans for you, my boy," he continued.

At this, young David struggled to free himself from Carter's grasp.

"Let me go! I want to go home!" David began to cry.

Alex walked over to the boy and kneeled down in front of him, "You think we're bad men, don't you? We're not so bad, you'll see one day. I hope you will see my place as your home and us as your family. I'm sorry, but you can never go back to your mommy and daddy."

Alex then stood up and addressed Carter, "Take the boy to my mansion and make sure he's cared for. Leave a couple men there to watch him, should he try to escape."

Carter took Alex aside so David wouldn't hear them, "Before I go, what is the status of the boy's parents?"

"Jason followed them to Paris. We don't know why they've gone there yet," Alex replied.

"What about the others?" Carter asked, as if to insinuate some of the protectors, like Eric Richards, may be out of their control.

Alex went back to his desk and sat down before continuing, "We know they are receiving assistance. Unfortunately we were unable to reach them before their helpers did. Carter, don't bother with that now, I have men on their way to take care of it."

Alex wanted to keep Carter focused on young David and out of unnecessary business. He was to start the boy's transition first thing in the morning.

Carter was hesitant with the orders he had received, "Don't you think the kid's too young for the transition process? Will he even live through it?"

Carter looked back at the small boy, who sat curled up in the corner of the room, his face wet with never ending tears. He knew better than to question Alex, but this seemed to be quite a stretch.

Alex answered firmly, "Yes, he will. Remember the boy's place. The master wants him prepared, nothing of the old David Richards must be left.

Only a blank, well-trained vessel will remain. It will be suitable for the master to inhabit, making him unstoppable and the most powerful of us all."

Then, Carter grabbed David by the elbow and dragged him back out of Alex's office. The two rode the elevator back down and got into a car parked in front of the building. The driver proceeded to Mr. Reuben's extravagant mansion on the outskirts of the city.

A Knight's Secret

It was a gray-covered sky that afternoon in Paris. Sara and I walked hand in hand up the front steps of the cathedral. The massive structure towered above us in all its splendor and rich history.

"Here we are!" Sara said, excited to look inside.

"I can feel it," I said softly.

"Feel what? Let's get inside," she smiled and pulled me along, as if she were a little girl again, anxious to board a roller coaster.

"I feel something divine," I continued, more nervous than excited.

Walking through the foyer, I could see several tourists doing what tourist do best, taking pictures. Others, more reverently, sat in the pews admiring the structure. One section of the building was blocked off by red velvet ropes and security guards. Beyond the ropes were three above ground ancient tombs.

I let go of Sara's hand and began walking to the other side, drawn by some kind of energy emanating from the middle tomb.

The guards watched me like a hawk as I stepped right up to the rope.

In front of the center tomb, a small placard had been constructed for the tourists' benefit.

It read, "Here lies Jacque de Molay, burned at the stake in 1314 A.D. The last Grand Master of the Templar Knights."

It was then that I realized whatever we had come here for was inside that stone coffin. Somehow, we had to open it. The obvious question was how? It was being heavily guarded and time was far too limited. The doors to the church would be closing soon. Sara had made a complete circle around the building and met me at the ropes.

"Have you found something?" she whispered, observing my focused demeanor.

"In there," I said quietly.

I used my head to point inconspicuously to the guarded tombs.

"But how?" Sara asked skeptically.

I walked back a few steps and began to think. I took out my trusted tape recorder. This was the same recorder I had been using in Brazil. I often used it to record the day's events, something I did up to four times a day. It had become more religious for sake of my boys after all these events had unfolded.

I sat down in a pew and hit record, "Boys, should anything happen to your mother or I, I hope these tapes find you.

I promise you won't be left with as many questions as I was concerning your grandfather's death."

I stopped the recorder as an uneasy feeling began to form deep inside me. Sara sat down next to me as we devised a plan. Our thoughts were quickly interrupted when we saw two men walk up to the security guards.

We watched intently as the guards handed their guns to the other two men and began to walk out of the cathedral. Was it a shift change? The new men were wearing black trench coats over their dress shirts and ties. Their eyes were covered by dark sunglasses.

I knew something was not right. No one else inside seemed to be aware of what was happening.

I turned to Sara, "Now's our chance, we need to hurry."

"What if they come back?" Sara asked, but I was already gone, making my way towards the front again.

As soon as I reached the roped area, I could feel the overwhelming evil rising from the two men.

"Let's not make a scene, Eric," one of them said.

"Jason," I recognized the menacing voice immediately.

I saw his evil grin and my anger quickly started ascending.

He spoke again, "Did you really think we wouldn't figure it out? I'd be careful if I were you. We're in a room full of pitiful tourists and you know we have no problem seeing them all die."

A few people were already staring at us, curious about what was going on.

Sara came up behind me, "Eric, what's going on?"

I held her by the waist and pulled her close to whisper in her ear, "Get the lid off that tomb, I'll take care of this."

Jason took off his sunglasses as his eyes and hands started turning black. At this, onlookers became terrified and bolted towards the exits, stampeding over each other on the way out.

"Eric, you've made this far too easy, now come quietly," Jason said.

"Never!" I shouted, as the energy within began building.

Jason was surprised by this, not having realized that Anna concluded my training. I could sense another evil being coming up behind me as though I had a second set of eyes. As he ran towards me, I quickly turned around and punched him with my left hand. On impact, it felt like hitting water. The energy discharged and the man was launched through two sets of pews. They blew apart in the center as he landed.

The other man standing next to Jason wasted no time in coming after me. He was faster than the other. He jumped to my left sideways and kicked my arms as I tried to block him. I instantly found myself sliding across the floor, striking a pillar. As I struggled to regain my bearings, I noticed something fall out of my jacket pocket and clink on the stone floor. I forced myself to sit up and reached blindly in the area of the fallen object. Grasping the intricately carved handle, I realized it was one of the short blades Anna had presented to me after completing my training.

Still sitting on the floor, the man who had kicked me was walking towards me. The look on his face was something I will never forget. The blackness within his eyes was not of this world, as though he were a marionette doll being controlled by Jason. He picked me up by the collar of my jacket, at which point

I plunged the ancient blade directly into his heart. Immediately, his grip loosened and I landed feet square on the ground. My hand was still firmly holding the handle when the blade slid out of his chest. The man fell to the floor as blackness filled the whites of his eyes.

As another one of his minions fell, Jason's anger began to rise. He shouted obscenities at the open church door. On command, another soulless vessel entered the cathedral.

"What are you waiting for? Kill him!" Jason ordered.

The man obeyed and lunged towards me. At the same time, Jason also bolted in my direction. With lightning speed, I spun around behind the man and stabbed him repeatedly in the back. He collapsed to the ground in front of Jason, who simply pushed him aside as though he were a piece of trash.

As Eric fought the evil ones, Sara was doing her best to concentrate on the tomb. She frantically searched the cathedral, looking for anything that would help her move the stone lid off the coffin. She spotted one of the poles that held up the velvet ropes. As fast as she could, she unhooked the latches from each side of the pole and dragged it towards the coffin. She lifted it up by the stand and used the pole like a crowbar to slide the lid off the top.

Underneath the stone lid of the tomb, laid the charred remains of Jacque de Molay. His garments were virtually dissolved, only his metal shoulder guards, chain-mail and sword remained untouched by the ravages of time. Sara studied the remains closely, as nothing of importance seemed to be inside.

Jason and I were still in the midst of our battle. With both hands thrust forward, a mass of energy erupted from Jason's finger-tips and launched me into the air. The force had burned a hole through my jacket and shirt, leaving a welt on my chest. The pain from the impact was unbearable, to the point where I couldn't even feel the hard, stone floor as I landed violently on it.

Sara began to scream, "Eric!"

She rushed over to me as steam lifted from my chest. I had come to rest next to another grave after having been tossed over what remained of the ropes. But, before Sara could reach me, Jason jumped nearly thirty feet forward, clearing the ropes. I laid there, eyes open but unable to move, as Jason stood in front of me. Sara didn't have time to react and was backhanded by Jason, sending her to the floor, unconscious.

Just then, when all hope seemed to be lost, the police arrived at the church. Jason was distracted long enough for me to get out of his sight. I limped over to the poll Sara had used to open the coffin. Jason continued to provoke the police to storm the cathedral. Wasting no time, I lifted the poll by its round base and ran over to Jason. Before he could turn around, I plunged the pole into the small of his back and out through his stomach. He dropped to the floor without so much as a word.

The French police were taken back at the sight of what they had just witnessed.

"Down on the floor! Don't move!" they shouted, guns drawn.

More officers rushed into the cathedral. I had no intention of going back to jail, we had come too far to have it end like this. I quickly clutched my blood-soaked hands into fists.

Before I could do anything, my mind flashed back to what Anna had said to me, "You must never hurt the innocent, Eric. No matter what happens."

Listening to the words of an angel, I calmed myself before my emotions could get the best of me. I improvised and directed the energy inwards. My first and only thought was how I hoped this would work. The officers became uneasy and afraid, as they should have. They watched in horror as the power, brighter than the sun, streamed off my necklace. The energy traveled to my hands and phased outward into a circle, three feet in circumference. Ribbons of piercing light could be seen moving like water around the otherwise transparent shield. As magnificent as it was, I was weak from battle and knew I couldn't hold the energy for very long.

The policemen fired every gun they had at my shield. The bullets dissolved on impact, as though they had struck pure acid. Millions of tiny metal flakes fell to the stone floor like confetti.

It was all a blur, but Sara and I managed to escape from the cathedral as fast as we could. But not before I glanced inside Molay's final resting place. I was fully convinced I was going to die and I didn't want it to be for nothing. I rushed over to the tomb while the officers were still distracted by their melting bullets. I instantly felt the divine presence resonating from the corpse's right hand.

Leaning over the coffin to get a closer look, I saw a gauntlet wrapped around the man's wrist. On the gauntlet was a design identical to my necklace. There was no second guessing myself, I stripped the gauntlet off the bones and hurried over to Sara, who was still unconscious. I secured the metal band inside my coat pocket and lifted Sara up into my arms.

With my shield still activated, I looked for a quick escape as the police fired until their clips were empty. Having no other options, they hastily rushed Sara and I, coming within inches of the force field. One unlucky officer touched the shield and was in turn knocked backwards. He found himself on the floor, convulsing in a seizure-like state, before his partners could drag him away.

I couldn't concentrate well enough to hold the shield and teleport out, so I let the force field fade out. An officer who had just arrived on the scene, had a full clip in his gun, but only managed to fire off two rounds. With Sara still in my arms, I spun around to protect her from the gunfire. The first bullet struck my shoulder while the other went into my thigh.

Before I knew it, we were both back in our hotel room. I was weak and exhausted. Struggling through the pain of the wounds I had suffered, I carefully laid Sara on the bed as my right leg buckled underneath me. I felt as though I had just ran a marathon. I didn't have the strength nor the focus to will the bullets out of my flesh or heal the wounds. I had to do it the old fashioned way. I grabbed one of my knives and a roll of paper towels and headed into the bathroom.

In front of the mirror, I proceeded to painfully remove the lead and dress my wounds with paper towels and duct tape. I nearly blacked out. Getting the bullets out was more excruciating than when they went in. I did my best washing up and grabbed a clean shirt from my bag, then headed into the kitchen in search of a pain reliever. The only thing we had was a bottle of wine Sara had bought from the restaurant downstairs.

I wasted no time self-medicating. Bottle in hand, I went back to the bed to check on Sara. She slept soundly, her hair draped over her beautiful face. All I could think about was how much of a mistake it had been to bring her here. I had nearly lost her today. The thought made me cry as I brushed her soft locks away from her eyes. I massive bruise on the left side of her once flaw-less complexion revealed itself.

"Come on babe, please wake up," I whispered in her ear.

There was no response.

"I'm so sorry, Sara," I continued.

I nudged her shoulder a little and she slowly began to come to.

"Eric? What happened? Did we get what we were looking for?" she asked, still groggy.

I immediately pulled her close in a loving embrace and kissed the top of her head. I was grateful she hadn't been seriously in-jured in the encounter with Jason.

"Honey, I'm okay. My face is really sore though," she said, gently pulling away from me.

She attempted to get up to look in the mirror, so I put my hand on her shoulder to stop her. She was still disoriented and didn't need to be walking around.

"You need to rest, you can look later. I'll run downstairs to the desk and get you something for the pain."

"Thanks, Eric," she said, forcing a smile.

When I got back to the room a few minutes later, Sara asked the inevitable, "What happened after? You look like hell"

I filled her in about what she'd missed of the battle with Jason and the French police, leading up to when we'd made it out. I presented the gauntlet and told her of its heavenly aura. The arm band possessed a connection to this divine source far greater than the one I wore around my neck.

We soon fell into a deep slumber that lasted well into the afternoon the next day. We hadn't realized how sleep deprived we were. We held each other all through the night, not wanting to ever let go again. I woke up when the sun finally broke through the windows, which revealed my wounds had been healed by the necklace while we slept.

My strength had also returned and I had an idea to try something. Sara had awakened to find me examining the areas where I had been shot in the mirror.

"Stay still for a minute," I said, walking back to the bed.

I took Sara's delicate face in my hands. Gently caressing her cheek bone, a small light began to emanate from my left hand. The light shined through my palm and turned a light pink against her skin. When the light faded, I pulled my hand away and saw that her bruise had vanished. The headache that had accompanied the blow disappeared as well. That day, we discovered I could not only heal my own injuries, but hers too.

We made love soon after, more passionately than we ever had in our marriage. The events that transpired in the cathedral had made us aware of the true nature of the situation we were currently in. Our time together was quite possibly limited and we didn't want to waste a single minute. I loved my wife, and in that moment, nothing else mattered.

The bodies of those who had fallen in the cathedral were wheeled down a long hallway, one by one, to the autopsy room. The last cadaver to be parked in front of the medical examiner was Jason. Police had preserved the scene and left the pole protruding from his stomach.

A male nurse began preparing charts for the victims that laid under the sheets. He was busy collecting information when Jason decided to end his death facade. Though badly injured, his strength would soon return.

Jason opened his eyes. Through the white sheet, he could faintly make out the silhouette of the nurse. He slowly began to move his arm down, the nurse still oblivious. He grabbed the nurse by the bottom of his shirt and tossed him out of the room, sending him flying back down the long hallway.

Jason ripped the sheet off himself and sat up on the gurney. He realized he was still impaled by the metal pole. Without hesitating, he gripped the pole and yanked it out of his stomach. A benefit of being one of the demoniacs was that he felt no pain. In seconds, the wound began to close and heal itself. He jumped off the gurney and made his way down the hallway.

He found the nurse, dazed, resting against the wall at the end of the hallway. The man saw Jason and in sheer terror, began to beg for his life. Jason bent down so he was eye level with the nurse. With one swift motion of his wrist, the nurse's neck broke in two. Jason nonchalantly stripped the man of his scrubs and put them on himself, then proceeded to stroll with ease out of the hospital.

Back in our hotel room, Sara and I were having lunch. Through bites of her panini, she examined the gauntlet. Puzzled, she took it into the kitchen to wash it off in the sink. Over the years, it had accumulated layers of dirt and dust. She believed the dirt however, was prior to Molay being placed in the coffin.

"That's better, now we might be able to see something," Sara said, satisfied with her makeshift restoration.

I met her in the kitchen to better examine the metal band under the light. We could see some type of symbol on the top and a small amount of writing on the bottom.

"It looks to be Gaelic," Sara observed.

She handed the gauntlet to me and the second she did, something strange happened. It was almost like the object retained the memories of all the men who touched it. The images flashed in front of my eyes so quickly, I could hardly make sense of them. I was at a loss until one memory I saw was all too familiar. It was the recurring dream I had been having months ago.

Everything was a match, except this time, it was from the woman's point of view. It played in reverse, from her death to the beginning. I could see her and the soldier together, making love. Then it flashed further back to before they met. Suddenly, like someone was pushing buttons on a tape deck, the images began to go forward. I saw a house, surrounded by Roman soldiers.

Inside the house were seven people sitting in the middle of the room, surrounded by several onlookers.

A highly respected, elderly man came out of another room, escorted by two more men.

The old man spoke, "It's time. May God be with you in strength and love, as you men and women fulfill your callings."

Then, the men who escorted the old man, unlocked and opened two chests. Inside the first chest were seven fabric gloves, all right handed. Each one had the same symbol on top, a circle with a cross in the middle. The second chest was opened to reveal necklaces of stone filled to the brim. The same kind my father had given me.

The seven of them followed each other to the chests where they each received their fabric gloves and stone necklaces. After the men and women had received their tokens, everyone knelt down to pray. At this point, every necklace and glove began to shine a brilliant white light.

The memories skipped forward again to the day of the woman's death. After she had passed, the soldier who loved her deeply, took the glove off her right. He would keep it in a safe place until he was told to pass it on. Later on, he would receive a stone necklace of his own.

Another flash and the images appeared further along. There were twelve men and women seated inside what looked like an abbey. One of the men was a young Templar Knight. Seven people stood up and stepped forward, where they proceeded to toss their fabric gloves into a fire pit. Once destroyed, the gloves were replaced with metal engraved bracelets, one of which I now held in my hand.

I saw several battles commence with the chosen seven. One great battle stood out, taking place on a lush, green hillside. Fighting in this battle were nearly one hundred men and women, wearing necklaces just like mine.

Then, as quickly as the visions had begun, they suddenly stopped.

"Eric?" Sara asked with concern.

"Yes?" I was slightly disoriented.

"You did that thing again, where you fall into a trance. It scares me when you do that."

"Sara, I think this gauntlet was trying to show me something. All of this, everything that has happened, goes back much farther than I ever thought!"

"Were you able to see anything useful?" she asked, taking the gauntlet from my hand.

"No, not really," I said, slightly discouraged.

THE DAY OF REVENGE

B ack in New York at Alex Reuben's estate, David Richards was being prepped for his transformation process. Carter gladly covered the boy's mouth with tape and strapped his hands and feet to a table. David laid there helpless, completely unaware of what was about to happen to him. The once inviting and cozy study on the first floor had suddenly turned into an unnerving atmosphere.

Carter was anxious to begin the transformation procedure, which would begin in a few moments. He selected a book off the shelf in front of the table that David was bound to. The book case opened, sliding to the left on a mechanical belt. It revealed an old, black stone archway, which was filled with a black, water-like substance. The liquid was in motion, moving vertically in the air.

"This is probably going to hurt for a few minutes, but you'll be fine after that," Carter told a terrified David.

Carter then unhooked the latch that held the metal table in a horizontal position. The table instantly flipped upright, forcing David to stare into the face of the black liquid. He attempted to scream, although the tape across his mouth stifled any sound.

As the young boy stared into the deep, dark water-like form, something started to happen, a stirring within. As the substance moved, it began to turn an even darker black. David struggled to free himself more and more with each passing second.

Then, as if on cue, Carter removed the tape from David's mouth as the blackness burst out of the archway, completely covering the boy. David immediately began screaming in agony from the pain the substance inflicted on his small body. While he cried out, the blackness moved slowly into his mouth and eyes. The substance then disconnected itself from its source, as though it were satisfied with its new host. As soon as it began, the process stopped, the remnants now possessing the boy.

Carter moved in front of David and unstrapped him from the table. The boy landed stiff on his feet. There was no expression on his face and no sound came from his lips. He stared straight ahead, completely motionless.

"Transformation complete. Now, on to your lessons, my young leader," the tone of jealousy rang out in Carter's voice.

Carter had served the cause for sixty plus years, expecting himself to be chosen for the task. Instead, this boy, who had done nothing to earn it, had been selected. Suppressing his envious emotions, he sat David down in a chair, as his motor skills would not return for a few hours.

The phone began to ring.

"Yes," Carter answered.

Alex Reuben was on the other end, "Is it done, Carter?"

Carter looked over at David, who was still staring blankly into the abyss, "Yes, Sir. David Richards is no more. He is a clean vessel, fully empowered."

"Good, your job is done. I will have someone else do the conditioning and lessons. In 10 years, the boy will become the man who will await our master's arrival."

Alex paused, thinking about what he would ask Carter next, "I want you to join your brother, Jason. I fear he has strayed from our purpose and has underestimated Eric Richards' abilities. You and I both know he's not as powerful as he believes himself to be. I can sense Jason is in grave danger if he proceeds alone."

"Yes, Sir, right away," Carter said promptly.

Putting the phone back on its base, he walked over to David. He picked him up and carried him to east wing of the mansion. In one of the many guest rooms, Carter laid the boy on a bed until the paralysis dissipated. He then followed orders and left Alex's estate in search of his brother, Jason.

In Philadelphia, the FBI arrived at Carla Munoz's home to relay information on the kidnapping of David Richards.

"This will only take a few minutes," one of the agents said.

Carla walked into the dining room and sat down at the table, followed by the three FBI agents.

"We've come to ask for your help, Ms. Munoz." the agent began.

"Gentlemen, I'm no longer with the bureau and this case has been nothing but a bad headache," Carla replied.

"I don't think you understand, Ms. Munoz. David Richards has been kidnapped, we're not giving you a choice. You will help us, or you'll be lucky if you can get a job as a meter maid in this city. I'm reinstating you and to show our gratitude, you will receive a bonus."

Before Carla's notorious temper could get the best of her, she reluctantly agreed.

"Why me?" was the one question she asked.

"You're the only one with extensive knowledge on the Richards case. We've reviewed your file and we think you have invested and sacrificed a lot for your department. Now back to the task at hand, we have already ruled out the boy's parents as suspects."

"What is it with this family?" Carla asked, shaking her head while looking down at her coffee mug.

"We're hoping you will help us answer that," the agent said.

The men stood up and began walking back towards the door, Carla followed.

The last agent out the door stopped and addressed Carla one more time, "I have one more piece of information that might provide you with a little motivation. Based on the description of the man from David's twin brother, we believe the kidnappers may have been responsible for your partner's death. However, finding the boy is still our number one priority."

With that said, Carla closed the door and sat down on the sofa. Her head fell to her hands as she began to cry, thinking of how much she missed Darren.

On February 3rd, 1986, the FBI and local law enforcement commenced a month long search for anything that would lead them to find my son, David. Nearly eight weeks had passed after his abduction, before Sara and I learned of it.

I took out my tape recorder to leave another message for Michael, "At this point, it has been three months since your brother was taken. We know who the kidnapper is, but against all instinct, we had to make the difficult decision to not seek him out. We could not return to America. This message is for you, Michael. Please do not hate us or be angry.

One day, you will understand that there was nothing your mother and I could do for David. Had we come home, we both would have been arrested and all of this would have been for nothing. Anna has also told us that she has seen your brother's fate and it was too late to save him."

The tape recorder clicked to a stop as the cassette reached its end. Sara placed the last of our clothes in a bag next to the bed, preparing to check out of yet another hotel.

"I guess that's it then," she said, staring longingly at a picture of our twins.

Anna had returned to us when she saw a vision of David's kidnapping. She was now standing by the window, deep in thought, gazing at the sun.

"Is it true, Anna?" Sara asked, breaking Anna's concentration.

"Yes, I'm afraid so. Most likely, it will be best if neither one of you return home. I'm sorry," Anna replied.

"But, we've been running from place to place for three months now, how much longer?" It seemed as though Sara was hoping for a different answer to the same question she had been asking on a daily basis.

"In two days, the others will finally be gathered together. They will then join us in Rome, in the exact location where this war started nearly two thousand years ago."

"I remember it!" I exclaimed, interrupting Anna.

Sara was surprised by my sudden excitement, "What do you remember?"

"I remember something else the gauntlet showed me. It took me back to the very beginning. Anna was there!" I said, pointing at Anna.

Anna smiled in response, "Yes, I was. It was a joyous occasion, a celebration full of friends and purpose. Most were in awe of being in such a wonderful presence."

Jason sat quietly in the darkness of his hotel room, which rested atop a strip club. In a fit of rage, triggered by something he couldn't even remember, he had snatched up one of the dancers. After dragging her upstairs, he had tossed her on the bed where he proceeded to strangle her with her own necklace. He now gazed upon the unfortunate girl, who laid lifeless on top of the hotel's cheap burgundy sheets, her long, brown hair covering her brown eyes.

Jason got up from the chair that sat next to the bed and made his way to the bathroom. In the hot shower, he washed off the blood left on his arms from the young woman's violent death. The water rushed over the countless scars that riddled his body, a history of many battles. His right shoulder showed cut marks for every guardian he had killed.

The most recent line was the thickest, only months old. This mark was for Fredric Richards.

While drying himself off and putting on a clean suit, Jason stared down at the deceased girl. He sat down next to her and brushed his fingers through her thick hair. A gleam filled his eyes. In that moment, he planned the day of his revenge.

After a moment of careful thinking, Jason decided to do something he hadn't done in many years. He rolled the girl over on her back, whose name, she had reluctantly told him before her death, was Crystal. Her eyes were still open in terror, looking up at the ceiling. Jason got on top of her.

"It's time you lived once again, my beautiful vixen. This time, you will have a better purpose."

Hovering above her, he opened his mouth and a black liquid oozed out and fell down into Crystal's mouth. A force left Jason's body and entered hers, bringing life back to the woman.

It was not often that one of the fallen would change someone and make them as one of their own. Jason was a fallen angel who inhabited the body he currently had. This woman however, was now only possessed by a demonic entity. The demon was never as powerful as its master. The summoning of a permanent demonic spirit could only be done twice in the course of a fallen angel's time on Earth.

As the life returned to her lips, Crystal began to scream uncontrollably. This was the evil spirit adjusting from the underworld to a living body. The demon would not completely claim the body, but would live in a symbiotic relationship with its host. Crystal's mind would have extremely limited access to the memories it gathered, proceeding the possession.

Just then, Carter walked into the room, "What have you done?"

Carter looked in disgust at Jason.

"We need her," Jason replied.

The girl laid quietly on the bed, staring off into nothingness like a zombie.

Carter gripped Jason's arm tightly, "Why have you been blocking my efforts to find you? Alex was right, you have become reckless!"

Jason shook himself from Carter's grasp, "I don't need you, any of you. I can take care of things myself, brother."

Carter walked over to the bed and sat down next to Crystal. He felt pity for her.

"You fool, Jason! If you do this alone, you could jeopardize all we have worked for!"

Controlling his anger and gathering his thoughts, Carter came to a compromise, "I won't tell Alex anything as long as we do this together."

Carter was enraged at what Jason had done, but he was still his brother. Carter knew Jason would be ended if Alex discovered what had been done to Crystal without permission.

Jason agreed to stay with Carter, and with Crystal, they would finish things once and for all the next day. They had already been aware of the gathering that would take place in

Rome, where they planned to ambush the group. To achieve the slaughter, Carter needed to call on the inferiors of that district. He did not want to take any chances on losing the element of surprise.

Both Carter and Jason knew there would never be another opportunity to find such a large group of guardians, like the one that would be gathering in Rome. It had been seven hundred and forty-five years since the last gathering of the heavens' chosen leaders. Alex was growing evermore impatient and certainly wouldn't wait another seven centuries if Carter and Jason failed again.

It was a warm spring day when Sara and I set out for Rome, with Anna by our side. I wasn't sure what had changed. I was led to believe we would be on this journey by ourselves, but I was ever more gracious that Anna had accompanied us.

Anna could hear the thoughts inside my head before I had a chance to give voice to them. I could never get used to it and it made me uneasy, not knowing whether or not my thoughts were private. Anna immediately addressed whatever entered my mind, which never failed to creep out Sara.

Sitting in the backseat of our rental car, Anna once again answered my concerns, "Eric, do you really want to know why the situation has changed?"

"Yes, my wife and I deserve to know what's going on."

"Well," her tone gave way to a dismal prospect for our success being slight to none.

Part of me didn't want or need to know what would happen to us. Sara was the one who wanted to know where we were going, who we were meeting, and when everything would happen. Her incessant schedule keeping was something that always drove me crazy, but I couldn't help but love her for being a little quirky.

Anna continued, "The enemy, you know as Carter and Jason, have broken ranks. They have gone off on their own, which means they have even abandoned their own natural instinct of survival. This makes both of them extremely dangerous. I fear they are intent on raising a sizable force to come after the two of you. Even with my help, without the others, you will surely die."

"Why are we driving there?" I asked, trying to understand her method of thinking.

"If we use our abilities now, they will find us. Like a homing beacon, they will pinpoint our location and follow us to our destination."

As Anna continued to talk, I looked at her in the rear view mirror. As I examined her expression, I could tell she was hiding something from us. When I had asked her about this earlier, she only said we would be better off not knowing.

A few hours later, we stopped at a rest area. Sara and I switched Anna for the backseat of our rental car. While we caught up on some sleep, Anna remained alert in the driver's seat, as angels had no need for sleep. I held my wife in my arms as she drifted off into a deep sleep. As I was about to do so myself, I looked up in the mirror to see Anna staring back at me.

"Everything okay?" I asked her.

With a puzzled look on her face, Anna finally answered, "I just wish I could understand, or better yet, know what it's like for humans to have the kind of love like the two of you share."

I was confused by what she was saying, "But, you're an angel. What could be greater than being in heaven forever?"

"Yes, but," she paused for a moment before continuing, "All I've ever known has been heaven, except for a few short visits. I'm always surprised by how often you humans take your gift of free will for granted."

Before I could think of how to respond to such a thing, Anna changed the subject, "Enough talking for now. Get some rest, you'll both need it."

The stress that had been weighing down on Sara and myself had definitely taken its toll on us. The few short hours we were able to sleep in the car had done wonders for us. Having Anna there, standing guard, made all the difference. That was the last day either one of us felt such peace and security.

THE GATHERING

We arrived in Rome the next day. Anna took us to an old building, where we entered through two sets of large wooden doors. The foyer was lined with stone tiles on the floor and renaissance-style paintings on the walls. We proceeded down a long hallway to the room where we would be meeting the others. The magnificent room had statues of Greek gods in each corner.

As we admired the architecture, three men and one girl came into the room to greet us. The men looked to be the same age as me, two with dark brown hair and one blonde. The girl looked to be no older than sixteen. She was shorter, with vibrant red hair and green eyes. As they walked towards us, one thing was apparent, all three men wore necklaces identical to mine. I looked for the little stone on the girl, but instead saw a glimmer on her wrist as the sunlight came through the window and reflected on the gauntlet she wore.

Anna had earlier informed us that of the seven gauntlets made and infused with power, three were constructed for female wrists. Was this young girl one of the chosen? As the four of them positioned themselves in front of Sara and myself, I could feel the extreme amount of power that radiated off the girl, like a fragrance without a smell.

The girl gave us both a hug and smiled, "We have heard a lot about you, Eric Richards."

Then, all four looked down at my gym bag in unison, as if they knew the gauntlet was inside.

"You've brought it! Very good! Did you have much difficulty retrieving it?" the girl asked, as though she wanted to see it.

"Just a little bit," I said with a smirk.

The young redhead glanced over at my wife, wondering why in the world she was there.

"May I speak with you in private, Eric?" the girl asked.

The girl was vastly more mature than her appearance led you to believe. Sara gave me the go ahead and said she would wait for me. The girl took me by the arm and strolled me over to the far side of the room, next to a glistening pool.

"Eric, why is your wife here? She has no part in this, not to mention the danger she is in simply by being here with us."

"With all due respect, she's my wife and she chose to be here by my side, despite the danger."

As I listened to what she had to say, I looked back at Sara, who was socializing with the rest of the group. I knew it was too late to convince her to leave. Truthfully, I didn't want her to leave. I couldn't have gotten this far without her.

In mortal danger or not, she would stay.

"You must be able to feel the change taking place," the young girl said, very unsettled.

I reassured the girl that I would protect my wife at all costs.

Her response was hard to accept, "These two gauntlets take priority over everything else, even your wife. If it comes down to it, we can't let them fall into the hands of the devil or all will be lost."

Just then I realized that each one of us, except Sara, could feel the change. It was best described as a cloak of darkness approaching within the spirit world. There was no longer any room for running. All we could do was prepare to stand our ground. We were stronger as a group. We couldn't let the evil ones divide and eliminate us one by one.

We walked back to join the others. Anna announced that she would not be with us in the eminent confrontation, but would stay close to observe.

"I will step in only if the situation becomes too much for you to handle," she explained.

Then she turned to me and gave me specific instructions, "Eric, do not forget, no matter what happens, if you feel the situation is out of control, I want you to run."

"Why?" I asked, thinking that running would be the worst thing I could do.

"Because you're the only one who can see the location of the final five gauntlets. That is your special gift, the reason you were chosen. If we lose you, we lose them and everything else."

Anna placed her hand on my shoulder reassuringly before turning back to the rest of the group, "May God be with each of you. May He protect you in the perils ahead. Should some of you fall here today, may He greet you in Heaven with open arms full of love."

With that, Anna walked out of the room. We all looked at each other, the feeling was mutual. I shook the hands of all the men and hugged the young girl before taking Sara in my embrace. She looked upset and she had every right to be. I kissed her like I had never kissed her before. She stared longingly into my eyes and nodded her head, as if to signal it was okay.

"For His glory and honor!" we said with hands together.

We started to file out of the room, knowing what would be waiting for us on the other side of the old wooden doors. The sun cut sharply on the masses going about their day in the square. Unfortunately, there was no time to warn the innocent of the danger about to befall on their small community.

The dark ones, as expected, had anticipated our arrival.

Three of them stood by the fountain in the middle of the square. Carter and Jason, along with a woman I had never seen before, had their hands clinched and their faces engulfed with anger. Jason had such deep-seeded hatred for me, his fists were literally shaking. Several others were scattered about the marketplace, pretending to be civilians.

I faced my wife and said, "I want you to stay here."

She attempted to protest, "I won't leave you."

"Just do it, Sara!"

Carter then spoke directly to the young red head, who was not as young as she seemed, "Tabitha, it's been what, 25 years?"

Tabitha chuckled, "The years have treated you poorly, Carter."

With an evil grin, Carter responded, "Enough with the small talk. Kill them."

Immediately, a dozen more minions surfaced from the crowd. I could feel the amount of tension with every bead of sweat that crossed my forehead. The mid-day sun was fierce. Even the light breeze was too warm for any kind of reprieve, as if to mock us. As I wiped the perspiration from my eyes, the dark ones began to form a semi-circle around us, offering no escape.

At that very moment, when I should have been by all rights terrified, I was surprisingly calm. Earlier that day, I had sat down to record one more message to my son.

"This may be my last recording to you, Michael. I had to tell you how it happened. Please don't be angry. Everything in this life has a reason. His will is perfect and loving, you must believe that."

The evil ones made the first strike against us. Tabitha fell to the ground, taking the first blow. Without hesitation, she shouted for the rest of us to fan out. We were to face them, one on one, rather than backed into a corner, as we were.

Quickly, the guns and knives came out. The evil ones wasted no time in firing straight at us, regardless of the fact that the area was swarming with pedestrians. They considered innocent people to be dead weight. We however, valued human life enough to further endanger ourselves to protect them.

Chaos and confusion rapidly erupted in the square, as the people frantically searched for cover. Screaming and crying, they fell like dominoes in the street as they were caught in the cross-fire. There were too many of the fallen to fight and even more civilians to protect at the same time. I attempted to hold up my shield of light in the form of a wall to protect them. Tabitha came to my aide and decided to blast a hole in the stone wall behind the people I was protecting.

I saw then just how powerful she was, in comparison with myself. Tabitha had dawned the gauntlet for decades, seeing that as the best way to protect it for the one who was destined to wear it. She raised it high in the air and spoke something I couldn't quite hear. No sooner had she finished speaking when a large pillar of fire broke through the sky directly above her, coming down upon the gauntlet. The gauntlet appeared to absorb the flame like a sponge, soaking up the power, leaving Tabitha unscathed.

"Move!" she yelled.

I directed the people to follow me and run behind her. The sweat falling from her cheek was visible, as it was taking extreme effort to hold the immense power. As soon as we had moved, the force was released, carving a hole through the stone wall. Rocks and debris fell to the ground as a huge cloud of sand circled Tabitha and filled the rest of the square. The ground began to shake and a sound, identical to a massive explosion, echoed throughout the village.

I used the cloud of sand as a diversion to evacuate the people through the opening Tabitha had created. Everyone was able to clear out before the sand settled and the battle continued. Without the distraction of pedestrians, the intensity level of the war had risen dramatically.

The battle would last nearly thirty minutes, although it seemed much longer. A constant barrage of strikes left some dead and the rest badly wounded. Jason and the woman by his side, whom I had heard be called Crystal, did not hesitate in attacking as soon as they spotted me through the dust. Before I knew it, Crystal appeared in front of me and grabbed my arm. We exchanged contact several times before Jason stepped in and violently kicked me into a nearby fruit stand.

Tabitha saw Jason had me on the ground, hand tightly around my throat. She ran over to my wife, who was hiding several yards away, watching in horror.

"Sara! The bag!" Tabitha yelled.

She was referring to the gym bag Sara and I had brought, which carried all the weapons. Sara had kept it at her side the whole time.

"Toss it here!" Tabitha continued.

As soon as the bag dropped in the dirt in front of Tabitha, she ripped it open. Finding two daggers, she sent them flying towards me.

"Eric!" she screamed, as the first blade hit Jason in the neck.

At the same time, I caught the second blade meant for me. Jason cried out in pain and foolishly loosened his grip on my throat. I maneuvered out of his grasp, blade in hand. As I jumped back, I pulled out the other dagger from his neck.

This was when I noticed something different about the evil ones, they didn't bleed red. Instead, blackness, similar to that of oil, poured out of Jason's neck. Once they had taken over a body, the need for red blood was gone. There was no room for any kind of good to flow through their veins. After a hundred years of inhabiting one vessel, the skin became no more than a covering for the darkness.

Jason, still kneeling on the ground, held his hand over his neck, preparing to heal himself. He yelled at the other dark ones to help him, even though they themselves were deep in battle. His orders were broken gargles, caused by the black liquid pouring down his throat.

"Forget about them, you imbeciles! Get Eric and Tabitha, they have the gauntlets!" Jason commanded.

Only two of Jason and Carter's men remained. Although outnumbered in the beginning, we had managed to even the odds. Without question, the current was strong and wide between ourselves and the heavens. Unfortunately, we had lost men too and by the end of the battle, only Sara, Tabitha, and I remained.

"Eric!" Sara screamed, as two of the dark ones launched themselves off a nearby building.

They were aimed straight at me.

With both blades in position, I ran towards them, determined to strike first. As they were still in mid-air, I jumped up and extended my arms. The daggers plunged into their hearts as all three of us fell back to the ground. With those two eliminated, Carter, Jason and Crystal were the only ones that still stood.

They barricaded themselves in front of me, intent on stopping me from finding the holy ground where five more gauntlets laid. These were the very pieces of the puzzle that would determine whether or not the world would be blanketed in permanent darkness or eternal light.

Jason slowly rose from the dirt and lifted his hand from his neck. The wound had healed and vanished while the black substance still remained.

"How foolish is your quest? You must know that we will succeed and reign this planet forever! Why throw your life away, Eric? What about your beloved Sara? Has she wronged you so badly that you would discard her life too?" Jason said slyly.

He pointed directly at me, his eyes began to glow.

"Get out of my head!" I cried out.

Jason had resorted to using his abilities to infiltrate my mind in order to weaken me. Tabitha grabbed my shoulders and shook me, desperately trying to distract me. My eyes became fixed upon the power. The pain was unbearable, I couldn't move. I stood paralyzed as the mental torture began to work.

"Eric!" Tabitha continued.

Her efforts remained unsuccessful to bring me out of Jason's psychological clutches. It was then that she noticed a trickle of blood cascading from my nose. She knew Jason would not stop until my brain was no more than mush. Sara watched in fright until she couldn't hold back any more. She ran towards me as my body fell to the ground. The necklace I wore, although powerful, could not protect me from an attack on my mind.

A Second Chance

"**B**aby, come back!" Sara shouted as she cradled her husband in her arms.

She began to panic and demanded Tabitha to do something quick. Tabitha could think of only one thing that would save Eric.

The angel, Anna, had been observing from the rooftop behind them. Tabitha looked up at her as if to say, 'save him'.

Anna spoke to Tabitha telepathically, "You know what this means, if I save him. I can only be involved twice. You won't be able to call on me again, this is my second time."

"I understand. Save Eric and I'll make sure he takes me to the gauntlets," Tabitha responded.

Anna leaped forward from the roof, her pale skin gleamed in the light as she emerged from the shadows. She appeared as an apparition eclipsing the sun before descending upon the town square. She landed with such force in the fountain, the basin broke in two, making the ground surrounding it shake like an earthquake. Cracks formed in the pavement and zigzagged like a spider web throughout the square.

Carter and Jason were unable to react in time to Anna's grand entrance.

Before they could even move, Anna used her powers to slow down time. She could have simply stopped time all together, but given her outstanding speed, she had no need to.

Anna rushed over to me and placed her palm on my forehead, magically breaking Jason's mental hold. My mind immediately displaced the evil power, which had attempted to destroy it just moments before. Tabitha had been the only coherent, unaffected witness to the happening. Wearing the gauntlet had rendered her untouched by Anna's ability. To Tabitha, from Anna's entrance to my healing, less than a minute had elapsed.

When time returned to normal, Anna turned to Tabitha, "Get Eric out of here. You'll have to use your strength, he's much too weak. I'll hold them off for as long as I can."

Tabitha nodded and without hesitating, helped me to my feet. Sara gripped me by the waist and threw my right arm around her shoulder. The two of them took me as fast as they could out of the open town square. I couldn't help but worry for Anna and wondered if I would ever see her again. I knew what saving me had meant. My thoughts came and went as my brain still suffered the effects of the attack.

My eyes became extremely sensitive to the intense sunlight while my temples began to pound like a bass drum.

Describing what I felt as a migraine would be putting it lightly.

"Come on, Eric, you've got to help me out here!" Tabitha stressed at our slow pace.

I struggled to hold my weight as my legs and feet began to drag across the ground. Tabitha and Sara exerted everything they had to carry me as fast as they could. I turned my head around for a moment to see Anna staring back at me. Our eyes met each other, but the way she looked at me was different. She did not speak to me through my mind, only silence prevailed. The little smile she sent my way said enough though. Just as I was nearly out of sight, I saw Anna resume the battle I had started. My last visual was Carter and Crystal being launched into a stone pillar.

I didn't know how the intense encounter would culminate for Anna. I did however, have the faith and confidence in God to protect one of His own. Could an angel die? If so, where would they go? Two days later, I would discover the outcome.

Anna was okay, being that she was nearly three times stronger than Carter, Jason and Crystal put together. She had kept this great strength by not being away from the source of her existence for more than six months.

Jason and Carter, on the other hand, had slowly become weaker by not seeing the gates of hell in more than 60 years.

To remain on an equal par with God and His army, a fallen angel is required to make a pilgrimage to hell once every 35 years. To do this, they must drain off their old essence and replace it with fresh spirit energy. The body which had been colonized, cannot survive without the fallen angel's presence for very long.

Jason and Carter had grown accustomed to their physical forms and didn't want to risk losing them for the added strength.

The rental car we used to travel to Rome was still parked three blocks from the square. Given the situation we were in, the distance seemed to be twice as far. Tabitha and Sara were reaching the point of exhaustion while all I wanted to do was collapse to the ground. This made it that much more difficult for them, as they were still dragging me along.

"I'm telling you this, Michael, so you know just how dangerous the evil ones are. Once we reached the car, I laid down in the back seat, my head on your mother's lap. I was altogether helpless, something I hope never happens to you. One minute I was my old self, completely fine. The next minute, according to your mother, the lights were on, but no one was home. The events of the battle were recorded in the Book of Eternal Life. Anna showed me its pages when she conducted my training. Someday, you will see it too."

We were traveling at great speeds in an attempt to escape from Carter and Jason. Luckily, local law enforcement paid no attention, I didn't know how that was possible. I did my best to relax and recuperate in the car, but every few minutes there would be a twinge in my head, more annoying than painful. It was similar to a small jolt of electricity.

My wife and Tabitha informed me later on that I passed out from the stress endured on my mind. I speculated that my brain had done that to protect itself, or the power from my necklace had done it for the same reason. Tabitha told Sara I was resting and not to worry. Even though we had just lost everything, we had somehow managed to win the battle in Rome. I was alive and because of it, there was still hope for the future.

"Sara, has Eric told you much about the gauntlets?" Tabitha asked, trying to distract Sara from the current state of events.

"No, I guess not," she replied, eager for Tabitha to continue.

"The location of the holy place where the remaining gauntlets had been stored, was lost even to those charged with protecting them. I think this was done on purpose so that if captured, the fallen couldn't invade the mind of a protector to extract the information."

"The one I wear was given to me to care for, a very long time ago."

Tabitha could see that the bumps in the road were jarring Eric. He had been in a deep, much needed sleep, for nearly ten hours. She was anxious for him to wake up and put Sara at ease. Tabitha's storytelling only distracted her intermittently.

"He's waking up!" I heard Sara say.

"Thank goodness," Tabitha said.

"How do you feel, honey?" my wife asked, brushing my forehead ever so lightly with her fingertips.

"My dear, I could not have woken to a more beautiful site than your smiling face," I replied with a smile.

In that instant, while being cradled in the arms of the woman I loved, I couldn't help but think about our family. Losing Dad was only the beginning. We would never see David again, while Michael must have felt abandoned.

"Am I a good father?" I asked Sara.

I wondered if I could have spared my sons from their certain fate by simply not having children.

"Honey, you need to stop tormenting yourself over David and Michael.

Not one thing could have changed what happened to them or us."

"That doesn't make it any less difficult, Sara."

I sat up and leaned against the door for support. Looking out the window, I tried to figure out where we were. The lack of trees and large number of houses pressed together made it look like a London suburb.

"Tabitha, where are you taking us?" I finally asked.

Before she could answer, I rifled off more questions, "Why does my head hurt so bad? What happened? The last thing I remember was the two of you carrying me across the street somewhere."

"Now, Eric just calm down. Everything is fine, we're all safe," Tabitha replied, glancing back at us through the rear view mirror.

She continued, "I'm taking you both to a safe place. The fallen won't be able to use their abilities to find us once we've made it inside."

"And my headache?" I asked again, still unable to completely open my eyes without pain.

"Jason got inside your mind, it's what he does best. Thankfully, Anna saved you. Your headache must be a residual side effect."

Then Sara spoke up, her eyebrows scrunched together in confusion, "What do you mean, must be? Have you not seen this before?"

"I have seen Jason use his abilities countless times before. But, only one other time have I seen someone survive. Your husband is beyond fortunate that Anna stepped in when she did. You owe her your life, Eric."

I knew Tabitha was right. Anna had saved me more than once. I owed her more than my life, if that was possible.

"Where are you taking us?" I asked again like a broken record.

"We are going to the Eluct da Selona in Kinsale, Ireland. It's translated as 'The Sanctuary' or 'Place of Protection'. Only four of these places exist in the entire world."

"I've been to one of them before. Anna took me there for my training," I was growing more curious as to why we were going to one now.

Sara raised the question before I could, "Why are we going there? Shouldn't we be retrieving the other gauntlets?"

"No, your husband is still too weak. All his strength was drained in the last encounter with Jason. This place is different, Eric, not like the one you saw. This one still has a vigilant blood-line of defense protecting it. It is the only place where you can get true rest and regain your strength. It holds a very unique and holy connection to the heavens and has been a refuge for more than two thousand years."

Then Tabitha took a photograph out of her pocket and handed it to me. It was a picture of the sanctuary.

"Wow, it's beautiful," I said in awe.

"A few faithful volunteers maintain the grounds," she replied as I handed her back the picture.

"I must admit though, it has been years since I was last there. I might need help finding it," Tabitha said nonchalantly.

Tabitha began acting strange when we arrived by ferry in Dublin. Every time our eyes met, she would immediately look away. We stopped at a gas station to refuel and pick up some quick snacks. Sara went inside to pay while Tabitha stayed outside with me. She glanced at me again through the back window as she stood by the pump. It was almost as though she knew something, a key piece of information, but was unable to tell me.

Sara returned to the car, a plastic bag in one hand and a notepad with directions to Kinsale in the other. She seemed to be in bright spirits. It melted my heart to see her so happy for the first time in weeks. I didn't know if it was because we were in Ireland, a country she had always wanted to visit, or that we were so close to our final destination.

Whatever it was, I hoped it would last.

"Tabitha?" Sara asked.

"Yes?"

"Not to doubt your years of wisdom, but why am I asking for directions when you've been there before?"

Tabitha was not pleased by my wife's question at all. I was curious to know the answer myself. Sara sat down in the driver's seat, offering to conquer the last three kilometers to Kinsale. We sat in silence, eagerly awaiting Tabitha's response.

Once we had pulled back on to the roadway, Tabitha finally spoke, "If you must know Sara, it has been sixty-two years to the day since I last stepped foot on this little island and a few things have changed. Highways like this one didn't exist back in the day. The republic had just been born and was already in the middle of a civil war. It was a chaotic time for everyone."

"Oh, I didn't realize," Sara said apologetically.

"Yes, I was actually born and raised in Sligo, until he found me. It was the summer of nineteen twenty-four, two weeks after my sixteenth birthday, when I met that monster known as Jason. After that, my life was never normal again."

Sara and I were both intrigued and horrified listening to Tabitha. I knew the story wouldn't end well the second she put Jason's name in it.

Tabitha continued, "He killed my family. Jason, along with his wife at the time, were thieves. They broke into my house and messed up by waking my father. Jason's wife was startled and not knowing what to do, she shot my father. To silence any witnesses, they also killed my mother and sister. I was able to hide under my bed, where I got a good look at them. I waited and watched Jason's wife for two weeks. I finally followed her into an alley and shot her dead."

"Days later, I met one of the faithful, whom I would never see or hear from again. He frantically told me I needed to take this gauntlet and protect it. I was to leave Ireland and someone would come and tell me what to do with it. As soon as I put in on my arm, I stopped aging like everyone else. I am getting older, but at an extremely slow pace. When I find the one who is meant to wear this gauntlet, I will return to normal"

"That same day, I discovered what Jason really was. His wife, however, was not like him. He had loved her so much, that he never put her through the transformation process."

Tabitha paused for a moment, "Jason has never forgotten. I took the last and only piece of humanity he had. Of course, he would have changed her eventually just so she could stay with him."

"Did you leave the country right away?" I asked, wondering why at sixteen, she hadn't just tossed the gauntlet.

"I left and swore never to return again. Today, I see things very differently. God, in His wisdom and mercy, has given us all a second chance at redemption. His love for me is still strong and that is why I no longer question Him as I once did."

"Did you ever have a family of your own?" I continued to pry.

Tabitha stared down at the gauntlet she wore. Her thumb glided over the engravings as a sadness enveloped her.

"There's never been any room to live or love like other people. And to bring someone else into this war wouldn't be right. I have all I need. If He sees fit to one day bring someone into my path, I would be most gracious," she replied.

Then, the sadness lifted and a soft smile formed on Tabitha's face, "With all I have lost, I would not go back and change anything. I have gained so much in living to see this, meaning you Eric."

"Me?" I said, surprised.

"Yes. You, whom God had chosen long before your birth, to bring the pieces back together for the first time in centuries. Humanity has been losing this war and you are here to give us a fighting chance."

Tabitha fell silent for the rest of the drive. She gazed out the window longingly, admiring the rain-soaked hills of Ireland. Although it was summertime, the sky was clouded over, producing a light drizzle. Despite the dreary appearance, the countryside was breathtaking.

Before we had continued our quest to Ireland, I was somewhat envious of Tabitha. The strength she seemed to possess made me think about indulging in the powers of the gauntlet I had retrieved in France. However, she held this mighty connection to the heavens at the greatest price. I felt pity and sadness for her now. I couldn't imagine wandering for decades alone, without family or anyone who would understand.

I opened my bag and looked at the gauntlet I carried. Sorrow overwhelmed me. I thought about the days before our lives had changed so drastically. What if I had chosen to walk away that day?

Sara slowly moved her hand and placed it on my knee, a worrisome look on her face, "What's wrong, hun?"

"Just thinking, that's all," I replied.

"I know how you like to over-analyze everything, Eric. You shouldn't do that, it just makes you depressed. Besides, we're almost at the end. Everything will be better soon, just like Tabitha said."

Korum Deo

The last leg of our journey was hard to navigate in the dark. I could tell that Sara was not sure of herself. We were on a small country road without any streetlights. Once we had left the city, it was beyond difficult to grasp a good visual on the landscape. The light drizzle had turned into a downpour, while the clouds had clothed the moon, diminishing the only ambient light we had.

"Eric, do you want to drive? I can't see a thing!" Sara said, finally giving up.

"Pull over, I'll see if Tabitha can help."

Tabitha had been dozing off with her head resting on the window. I gently nudged her as Sara carefully pulled off to the side of the road.

"Why did you wake me? I know we're not there yet. I would have felt His presence," Tabitha said in a groggy tone, clearly not pleased.

Tabitha reached over the seat and yanked the keys out of the ignition and handed them to me. She looked angry as she closed my fingers over the keys.

"I'm disappointed in you for waking me out of my communion with the father.

You could have handled this yourself, Eric."

"I thought you were asleep!" I was confused.

She went on to explain what she meant by 'communion with the father'. Joined with all the faithful who take part, Tabitha fell into a catatonic state. This 'communion' was not conducted often as it left the participant extremely vulnerable.

"Is that why you're bringing me to the sanctuary?" I asked, having already figured out the answer.

When Tabitha said I needed some sleep, she meant a different kind of rest.

Sara and I got out of the car to switch places as the rain drenched us from head to toe. Before I stepped back in the car, I looked behind me into the darkness. I felt a presence of pure hatred. Although it was only for a split second, the sensation was strong.

"What are you doing? Get in the car!" my wife shouted from inside.

While I held the driver's side door open with my left hand, what had seemed like only the blink of an eye, had apparently been longer for Tabitha and Sara.

Searching the darkness for a source of the presence, I knew it was Alex and another dark being. I couldn't see anyone, but I could almost visualize them in my mind.

The other figure accompanying Alex was so full of evil, it was as if it were the devil himself.

"Come on, Eric!" Tabitha yelled, growing extremely impatient.

I snapped out of it and got in the car.

"I don't see how me driving is going to be any better," I said.

Tabitha grabbed the necklace I still wore and held it directly in front of my eyes, as if to exaggerate her point.

"Use this, Eric. Concentrate," she responded in a sarcastic tone.

She seemed so confident, and her faith in me was something I couldn't quite understand.

She continued, "Believe. Look through the darkness."

Then, Tabitha placed her left hand on the amulet and said something that would stay with me in my darkest hour, "Our strength is our faith."

There, on the side of that desolate road somewhere in Ireland, I began to believe in the impossible. It felt almost like a slow rising heat over my eyes. They began to burn as a sense of fear emanated from deep within.

"What's happening to me?" I asked, my voice shaking.

Sara placed her hand on mine and was shocked to see my eyes were glowing.

"What are you doing to him?" she cried out.

Tabitha remained resilient, "Eric, the pain will pass in a minute. If you fight it, it will only take longer. In your veins, runs the blood of more than a dozen faithful believers, who have been right where you are now. They have felt the battle between the carnal mind they had known all their natural lives and the true, untarnished, heavenly one."

The night soon became as bright as day. I could see every living thing as though it produced its own light, through its own life force. The fields and trees, even Sara and Tabitha, shined brilliant like the sun.

As the rain slowed to a light drizzle, my eyes began to acclimate.

"Now you see the world like the father and His angels do!" Tabitha's eyes gleamed as she remembered her first time seeing the light, many years ago.

Tabitha's words comforted me, enabling me to use my new found ability to guide us the rest of the way. I reassured Sara I was okay, then pulled the car back onto the highway.

The last thirty minutes of our journey felt more like three hours to me. My eyes were constantly readjusting to the variances in light from one object to another. I could see the white glow from my eyes reflecting off the steering wheel, which was somewhat distracting.

Somehow though, we finally made it to Kinsale.

It took no time at all to find St. Multose Church. Everything was dark except for the church. I could almost make out a lake or river on our left. Perhaps it was part of the ocean. There was no mistaking, however, the beam of light shining down from the heavens, onto the church. Still, I was the only one in the car who could see it, so there was no point in trying to describe it.

"How do I return my sight back?" I asked Tabitha.

Tabitha looked annoyed, assuming I already knew the answer.

"Concentrate on those you love, and believe," She said firmly.

The way she emphasized the belief in the power of love, showed me that even though she didn't have someone special in her life, she still knew such perfect love. I did as I was told and thought of my beautiful wife and my boys, whom I desperately longed to see. Slowly my vision returned to normal and the bright beam of light above the church vanished.

Sara spoke up, "Will we need our gear?"

She referred to the two gym bags in the trunk, loaded with our weapons.

"We'll bring them with us as always.

We can't be too careful. If just one gauntlet falls into the wrong hands, we might as well surrender the others," Tabitha replied.

As we left the car and started walking up the stone staircase to the sanctuary doors, Tabitha looked at me, "Did you feel that?"

We had both nearly been knocked off our feet by an unfamiliar force.

"I did. What was that?" I asked.

Tabitha was as confused as I was, "I'm not sure, but it definitely came from the north."

Sara had apparently been unaffected by the quake-like force and stepped back from the doors to make sure I was okay.

Just then, the door to the sanctuary opened and a figure of a man dressed like a priest emerged from the shadows.

He spoke softly, "You must be so cold. Please, come inside and dry off those clothes."

The three of us accepted his invitation and stepped over the threshold.

The old man spoke again, "I'm Father Connolly and I have been expecting you for quite some time now."

His words were so peaceful, immediately putting me at ease. The sanctuary was small, but still beautiful. Sara held my hand as we walked around the building, admiring the architecture and paintings which adorned the walls. Father Connolly educated us on the history of the church and the purpose it served.

"I have been here for some time now. As first protector of Ireland, my instructions were simple, to provide rest and protection to any of the faithful for as long as I could," Father Connolly explained.

We stood silent as we consumed this new information. Being exhausted from the trip and drenched from the rain made the current circumstances overwhelming. Father Connolly seemed to read our minds and brought his history lesson to a close.

"Let me show you to your quarters. You must need some rest after your long journey," he said.

The priest escorted me to my room. He insisted, in God's most holy house, that Sara and Tabitha sleep in another room.

"In this place, you have come to find Him and His guidance. This can only be done with the absence of all distractions," Father Connolly explained.

I hung my wet clothes up to dry and opened a small dresser drawer in search of something warm to wear. There were only dark red robes inside. I smiled, thinking that they looked a little outdated, but at least they would be warm. I took one out and wrapped it around myself, diminishing the chill. I sat down on the bed, and fished through my bag in search of my recorder.

"Hello son. I leave you this message in the sanctuary. It has been a long journey for your mother and I, but we finally made it. I received a glimpse into what I can only call a test of faith. I must follow through, our end objective is very close. I love you, Michael."

Laying there in the dark, with only the flickering of the candle-light, I spoke into the recorder until there was no tape left. I began to doze off, feelings of excitement and fear filled my heart. The future for David and Michael rested in my hands.

Rectified

A knock on the door came early the next morning, interrupting my dream. It was more of a vision, showing me our next destination. I pulled the plush robe around me and walked to the door. To my surprise, Tabitha was on the other side, already dressed and anxious to start the day.

"We have to be quiet," she said, inviting herself in and closing the door behind her.

She sat down on the edge of the bed. Although I was still half asleep, I could clearly tell something was troubling her.

"The sun's barely up, what could be so important that you have to wake me now?" I asked.

I started to open the door again, implying that I wanted her to leave. I desperately needed a couple more hours of sleep.

"Wait, Eric please," she said.

"You've seen it, haven't you? That vision I had last night, you saw it before me, didn't you?" I asked.

"Yes," she replied, looking down at the floor.

Tabitha had that same look she'd carried at the gas station. Only now, I knew the reason for it.

She stood up and came close to me, so close, I could feel her breath on my face.

"It's not a coincidence that I'm here with you now. We must consider ourselves fortunate to be chosen by Him and not be fearful. Each one of us are a piece to this puzzle, regardless of how long we must wait for the rest to find their place. Our place is here and now. I will stand and fight, but we are stronger together. You must not forget though, that even in the darkness, you are not alone."

I hung on Tabitha's every word, waiting to see where she was going.

She continued, "The priest has been involved in this war longer than any of us. Because of this, he has been known to fight for both sides. I'm afraid he will betray us. Eric, we must leave now."

Tabitha's concerns were sincere, I could feel the torment in her voice. I reluctantly agreed to leave the sanctuary, although we had gone through so much to find it. We decided to leave quickly after breakfast, but not too quickly as to raise any suspicions.

"You're sure Father Connolly would do such a thing? I felt no sense of evil in the man," I said.

"No, I'm not sure, but I don't want to stick around and find out," Tabitha responded, while helping me pack my bags.

I opened the door to the hallway to see that Tabitha already had her bags packed.

They were neatly lined against the wall. I set mine down next to hers.

She met me in the hallway and picked up one of the duffel bags, "I'll go first and take this to the car. We shouldn't go at the same time. You can grab yours after breakfast."

I nodded in agreement.

"Alright, let's go."

"Okay, I'll go wake up Sara," I said, starting down the hallway.

Tabitha caught me by the arm.

"What?" I asked, confused.

"You know, Eric, we don't have to bother Sara. She doesn't need to go with us, you've seen what happens."

The look Tabitha gave me spoke volumes of pain she'd been all too familiar with. She could not have tried harder to spare us of this pain.

"No prophecy is ever set in stone, that's what Anna told me. We will continue this journey together. I'll never leave her side again," I explained to Tabitha.

She gazed at me as though she really didn't understand why I wouldn't spare my wife such agony. She didn't attempt any rebuttal. Instead, she nodded and carried her bag down the hallway.

I found Sara's room and quickly and quietly tried to wake her up. I knelt down beside her bed and gentle shook her shoulder. She looked so peaceful, deep in dreamland, it was hard to have to wake her up.

"Honey, we have to get going," I whispered in her ear.

"What smells so good?" she asked disoriented, referring to the rashers and eggs cooking in the kitchen.

I smirked, my wife was too cute, "Let's get dressed and find out."

Unwillingly, Sara got out of bed and began searching through her bag, looking for clean clothes.

"Eric, we just got here. Why are we leaving now?" she asked while pulling a sweatshirt over her head.

I reached for her jacket on top of the dresser, "Because Tabitha doesn't trust Father Connolly."

Sara looked blankly at me, as if to say, "Is it always up to Tabitha?"

"It's okay babe, I know where we are going. I saw it in my dream last night. Today is the day," I told her, trying to give her some comfort.

"We get there today and this is all over? We can go home?" Sara said, although in her heart, she still had her doubts.

I held her in an affectionate embrace while we stood in the doorway. I did this with hope and peace rather than fear.

No matter what could happen, our destinies had been woven together from the moment we laid eyes on each other, so many years ago.

"No regrets?" I asked softly.

"Not for a second, forever is forever," Sara replied with a smile.

I took her hand and we began walking down the hallway, towards the kitchen and near the wonderful aroma of breakfast. As we passed by the front door, we noticed Tabitha and the priest in deep conversation. I nudged Sara to keep her moving, despite the fact that we both wanted to know what was being said. Had Tabitha been caught by Father Connolly? Did he discover our plans to leave without his knowledge?

In that moment, I remembered Anna telling me that I couldn't fully trust anyone.

"Some evil is obvious and you can feel it in your heart. Other evil is like that of a wolf, hidden in sheep's clothing, searching the land for innocence to devour," she had told me.

The thought of a corrupt man of God lingered in my mind as we sat down at the breakfast table. A young man, no more than fifteen years of age, placed a magnificent spread of food in front of us. He then proceeded to dish out heaps of scrambled eggs and rashers onto our plates.

The young man spoke only a few words, "I hope you enjoy your breakfast. This kitchen isn't meant to accommodate many guest. Welcome, my name's Phillip."

"Thank you, Phillip. Everything looks delicious," Sara said.

Earlier, Tabitha was making her way back from the car. She had loaded the duffel bag containing the weapons and the precious gauntlet. After walking up the steps, she was stopped at the door by Father Connolly. He had opened the door before she even had the chance to turn the knob.

She quickly found herself in a bad situation and was not one to be caught off guard.

"What are you up to?" the priest asked.

"I was getting some of my personal things from the car. Is that alright with you?" Tabitha said as she pushed Father Connolly aside.

As soon as she passed the threshold, the priest grabbed her by the arm. As he halted her, a small, powder foundation case and lipstick tube fell to the dark, wooden floor.

"Satisfied?" Tabitha asked sarcastically as she went to pick them up.

After securing her belongings in her purse, Tabitha turned to address the priest again, "You may think you have everyone else fooled Father, or should I say Liam, but not me.

Just because you have done many righteous deeds, does not make you righteous by any means. Nor does it make up for things which placed you here, bound to His service."

Once Phillip had returned to his kitchen duties, leaving Sara and I alone, we quietly walked towards the dining room door. Placing our ears intently against the wood, we could hear the conversation between Father Connolly and Tabitha at the front entrance.

We were able to hear the last words Tabitha spoke, "I kept your secret for all these years because of what you did for me in the beginning. I'm forever grateful for that Liam, but don't look at me like we are the same, I'm nothing like you. I see inside, just as He does, and you still need a change of heart."

Then we heard Tabitha's light footsteps approaching us and we rushed back to our seats. Phillip had returned to refresh the dishes and looked at the two of us as though we were lunatics. Thankfully, the poor boy was obviously clueless.

Tabitha burst through the door, still fuming from her unpleasant conversation, but doing her best to mask it. Phillip was instantly startled and nearly knocked over the glass he was pouring water into. He finished making his rounds of the table and once again excused himself hastily.

Tabitha sat down and joined us for breakfast, "What's wrong with him? That boy is just wound too tight!"

It was ironic hearing Tabitha speak down to the young boy, as she looked no more than sixteen herself. Her irritability quickly dispersed as she leaped into her plate of scrambled eggs as though she were famished.

Sara and I had decided prior to Tabitha's arrival not to mention what we had overheard earlier. It didn't seem to make a difference anyways, we already had plans to leave.

"I'll take your plate honey," I said to Sara as she sipped her coffee.

"Thank you," she smiled and placed her empty plate on top of mine.

I walked into the kitchen, leaving Sara and Tabitha to their girl talk. As I placed the dishes in the sink and began to run the water, I became lost in the moment. The question that not one of us knew the answer to, loomed in that kitchen. What would happen after we finally retrieved the artifacts? The chances were pretty good that the three of us would not arrive before the fallen did. If that were to happen, what would we do then?

I stared out the small window over the sink for what seemed like an eternity. The fog was radiating from the lake that joined with the Irish coast. I was so deep in thought, I didn't even notice the sink beginning to overflow.

"Hun? Eric?" Sara said.

She repeated herself about four more times before her words broke through the myriad of thoughts swarming around my brain.

"Sorry, I got distracted," I finally said, as the water seeped over the side and onto the floor.

Phillip had returned just in time to see the small pond I had created. He looked completely flustered, but without a word, went to the closet to find a mop. Seeing it was best to stay out of his way, Sara and I returned to the dining room. Tabitha was nowhere to be found.

"We have to go," Sara said.

"I know. Tabitha said it would be best to split up here. I'll go with her and you can follow us," I replied.

Sara smiled in agreement in an attempt to hide her fears from me.

"But, Eric, we only have one vehicle."

She hadn't seen me swipe the keys to Father Connolly's van.

"Got that covered," I tossed her the keys and nodded my head in the direction of the van.

I kissed my wife and told her I loved her once again. I didn't want to leave her. She had already done so much for the cause. It gave me some comfort knowing she was a strong, relentless woman.

As quickly and quietly as I could, I obtained my bag from the hall and started down the stone steps. Tabitha was waiting for me in the car, apparently annoyed as though she had been waiting for far too long. Not a sound was made between us as I hopped into the driver's seat. In fact, there hadn't been a single sound or movement from anywhere.

The rain had dissipated and only a slight mist in the air remained. Fog was gliding gently across the stone pavement. All was still, but the peaceful nature of the Irish hills would not last long.

"Eric, let's go!" Tabitha commanded.

Day of Days

None of us could have foreseen the events that were about to happen. The fallen had been waiting for us all night just down the street from the sanctuary. I was the only one they wanted. They were quick to discard Tabitha, pulling her out of the car and then dragging her across the asphalt. With a single fluid motion, she was then tossed across the street.

Sara didn't even have a chance to get her foot on the gas. A man sitting in the backseat revealed himself to her.

"Don't," the stranger said as he turned the ignition off and propelled the key out the window.

Satisfied with Sara's helplessness, he then jumped out of the van and sprinted towards me. He yanked open the passenger's side door and sat down next to me. I was not familiar with this man. However, it didn't matter, I knew what he wanted and where the situation was headed. He did not hesitate in jabbing the barrel of his gun into my ribs.

"Mr. Reuben is anxious to have this current state of affairs resolved."

By this, I knew he meant the destruction of the gauntlets and ultimately, my death.

"Drive now!" yelled another man, appearing in the backseat.

The two men were similar, but unlike the demons in Alex's army. They were not fallen angels, but possessed humans tasked to do Reuben's dirty work.

Moving as fast as possible, I weaved in and out of traffic. Our destination was Cashel in the county of Tipperary. The rise of a new hope or the destruction of our world would be decided there.

Some ten minutes had passed before Tabitha could lift herself off the hard pavement. She rushed over to Sara, who had also been violently thrown to the ground.

"Are you okay?" Tabitha asked, helping Sara to her feet.

"Yeah, I think so," Sara replied, disoriented.

"They took Eric. Did you see which way they went?" Tabitha continued.

Sara shook her head. Neither one of them had any idea of where he had been taken. Luckily, Tabitha knew the location of the gauntlets from her joined vision with Eric the night before.

The two women wasted no time in searching the rain-soaked shrubs for the keys to the van. Sara frantically combed through the grass, anxious to get her husband back.

"I can't believe he's gone!" Sara cried hysterically.

"Calm down, Sara, we'll find him."

"How can I possibly stay calm? My husband has been kid-napped!"

"Found them!" Tabitha shouted, holding the keys up in the air.

They raced to get into the van and peeled out, back onto the highway. Leaving Kinsale in their rear view mirror, they sped towards the town of Cashel.

There was a stillness in the air, unique to that day. It was as though all the noise in the world had simply been sucked out of the environment. The planet, and all the people inhabiting it, moved on like any other day, unaware of the events that were about to take place.

I passed every car I could on the motorway as the gun be-came evermore present in my side. The man roared at me every few minutes to drive faster. At the end of his words he would add a jab to my ribs with the barrel, as if I hadn't already gotten the point.

The man in the backseat sat silent. His presence was no doubt meant to keep me in line, should I attempt to escape their ride of fate.

Did these pawns of Reuben not know that such force was unnecessary? If we arrived at Cashel without the escort, the out-come would result in the same confrontation.

The rain returned with might, blurring the taillights in the car ahead of me. Finally, I spotted a sign on the right for Tipperary and Cashel.

Thirty minutes behind Eric, Sara worried frantically about her husband.

"He's tough, mentally, spiritually, and physically. I've never met anyone stronger. As long as they still need him, nothing will happen to him," Tabitha said, attempting to reassure Sara.

Sara knew in her heart that Tabitha was right. Despite the fact, she felt little comfort in Tabitha's words. No matter how powerful Eric was, she would not let her husband do this alone.

The highway faded as the two women approached the county of Tipperary, within an hour of Cashel. There was no turning back now, although Tabitha and Sara would never think of fleeing. The three of them had experienced too much together already and they weren't about to part ways.

As Tabitha sped down the highway, desperately trying to make up time, Sara sat silently in the passenger's seat, praying, "At least I have comfort in this: you wanted to make a difference all your life, Eric. This is your chance, my dear husband. My only prayer is that you sense my words and faith in you."

"Please God, do not let anything happen to him before we can see each other again. Eric needs you now, above all else."

I knew it was useless to reason with my captures, but I didn't have very many options. I wanted to understand why ordinary humans, like these two men, would serve the devil's right hand man. How had Reuben managed to lure them in and then have them agree to a possession?

I glanced at the man to my left, then in the rear view mirror at the man in the backseat. I needed to break them or at least attempt to weaken them mentally. I stared back at the road in front of me and collected my thoughts.

"Gentlemen, I can tell you're obviously not the usual mindless slaves that Alex Reuben typically employs. What did he promise you in return for your service? Great wealth? Yes, it must have been untold riches in exchange for the destruction of the world. Or maybe I'm thinking too small. Perhaps he promised to deem you kings in the new kingdom of darkness."

Not to my surprise, my efforts did not infiltrate their controlled souls. At least with the mindless demoniacs I had encountered before, it was a simple kill or be killed scenario. These two were still able to keep most of their own thoughts.

"Shut up and keep your eyes on the road!" the man to my left shouted, while further pushing the barrel into my side.

The man in the back finally spoke, "When we arrive at the Rock of Cashel, you will drive to the south side of the castle."

With that a thought entered my mind, something that sent chills down my spine. How many civilians did Alex have as his hired hands of destruction? Were some of them unaltered, void of any possession? Were they simply volunteering to be traitors to the human race? I recalled all the people I had come into contact with since Anna had opened my eyes. Had any of them pledged an undying allegiance to the devil, secretly serving the other side?

I knew one thing was for certain. These two pawns of Reuben's would never see the riches or power they were expecting upon completion of their mission. The empty promises were easily swallowed by ignorant sheep full of envy. Most likely, every unfortunate individual recruited by Alex, Jason, and Carter, would be gathered up and slaughtered. Every soul would be damned to an eternity in hell. Before this could happen though, Reuben would extort every bit of usefulness out of them.

The town of Cashel was a small community, dwarfed by its massive castle. It stood proudly, showcasing the dedication of those who had built it centuries upon centuries before. I was humbled to be able to lay my eyes upon it.

"How many times did your walls of stone see the arrows and swords of evil men?" I thought to myself.

As we approached the magnificent wonder, I could feel its power and all its glory. The future rested in the hands of so many men and women who had sacrificed everything. This place had been chosen for them, named the holiest and most fortified castle in all of Ireland at the time. Should we fail, their sacrifices will have been in vein.

I knew once inside, I would be outnumbered. Through all this, there are moments that still feel like a bad dream. Driving up to the castle and knowing what was waiting inside was one of those moments, the kind of nightmare you only half want to wake up from. There's that small part of you that always wants to see what happens.

The ominous sky did not shed any light on the events to come. The rain did not let up, like a fighter in the ring, beating back the sun. If I succeeded, the rain would eventually have to surrender and let the sun prevail.

We choose our own desires in this life. I knew, without a doubt, our paths had been laid out before us. Sara and I may not have chosen this for ourselves, but we made our decision and stood firmly in it together.

I drove through the south entrance and parked at the outer wall of the castle. The first chance I could get, I would make sure these men didn't walk away for hurting Sara and Tabitha.

To our right, I saw a stone statue adorning the archway at the entrance. The figure was that of the mother Mary. The rain flowed down her face like a river of tears. Her appearance only added to the already foreboding atmosphere.

As soon as I got out of the car, my wrists were handcuffed in front of me. Before they could wrangle my arms though, I caught a glimpse of an officer's badge on one of the men. My first thought was that it had to be fake, allowing the dark ones to possess immunity and means. Then I realized it was quite possible that Alex's reach ran far deeper than I could have imagined. The devil himself was a crafty and tricky bastard, sinking his claws into anyone who would allow him. How could we defeat an evil that seemed to have no boundaries?

The cuffs were tight. I focused on the castle, admiring the sheer majesty of it, doing my best to ignore the uncomfortable bracelets. My moment of zen was interrupted by a violent blow to my stomach. I fell to one knee into the mud, as rain and darkness drenched me to the core.

"Alex said he'd put up more of a fight than this! I don't see what the big deal is, Eric Richards ain't so tough!" one of the men laughed.

I was then grabbed viciously by the arms and lifted up off the ground.

"Still, as a precaution we should take some of the fight out of him."

"We can't kill him though, we promised Alex Reuben he could have the honors."

I began to space out, having no interest in knowing the details of how I was about to be tortured. I prepared myself for a world of pain, just as the first fist hit my stomach. My hands were still cuffed as the two men took turns beating me. My shirt was torn off my shoulders, as their fists landed against my cold body. Each strike forced me backwards, but I remained silent, only wincing at the repetitive torment. Blood fell from my brow and lips, mixing with the rain to make a steady, red stream of liquid glide down my body.

There was no trace of hesitation in the men, as they continued to wale on me. Through smiles and laughter, they taunted me, testing the boundaries of my strength like never before. In that instant, I could feel the eyes of every demonic spirit in attendance. Their presence cast in pure joy at the momentous occasion of my falling.

Searching deep inside myself, I tried to muster the strength to rise up. I was far too week at this point though. There was only one thing I could think of.

"Don't forget you need me alive," I told the men through half mutterings of pain.

I glanced up at them with a swollen and bloodied face. Judging by the look on their faces, they had apparently forgot to leave me breathing. If anything happened to me before I located the gauntlets, these men would be tortured themselves to no end. I could see the prospect of agony weighed heavily on their minds, allowing me a reprieve from the beatings, at least for now.

I didn't know at the time that Carter was nowhere to be found in Ireland. Instead, someone else had decided to go rogue and steal the spotlight. This mystery man appeared as a shadowy figure, emerging from behind the wall to our left.

"Looks like someone's been having all the fun without inviting me to the party!" the voice was eerily familiar.

The man was tall and wore a black trench coat and black leather gloves. His face was concealed with a mask, only revealing his eyes.

"Stop! Move and we'll kill you!" my oppressors shouted, I was now the least of their problems.

The masked man chuckled, clearly amused by the threat.

"I can't have you delivering my prize!" he yelled back at us.

Before the men could respond to the new intruder, the masked man opened his right hand and abruptly made a fist. The men next to me immediately clasped at their chests, screaming in pain. They fell lifeless to the ground, blood seeping from their lips. Their hearts had literally been crushed from the inside.

Who was this mystery man? Was he a friend or enemy? I would find out soon enough. One thing was for certain though, this man could kill in the blink of an eye. My fate now laid in the hands of a complete stranger.

The man grabbed my arm and looked me directly in the eyes, as though he were looking for a sign of consciousness. I knew at that point there would be no relief from the pain. This man was not a friend, I could see it in his eyes.

"Did you pass out on me? You, Mr. Richards, will witness my rise, just before I kill you," he said with great pride and assured victory.

Then, he slowly lifted the mask from his face, revealing a large scar across his left eye, which was also blinded. I assumed he had been using his abilities to hide this imperfection for many decades, after sustaining it from a previous fight.

Jason now stood before me, grinning.

"You knew today was coming, if not me, it would have been the others. You can't fight fate forever, Eric!"

HOPE AGAINST HOPE

The rain fell consistently, washing the dirt from my bloodied body. I remained silent, standing next to the car, keeping my eye on Jason. There was no use in talking, it would have been like trying to reason with the devil himself.

Without a word, Jason grasped the amulet around my neck. It was the same necklace that had been with me since the beginning, a gift from my father. He violently ripped it off my neck and tossed it to the ground.

"Move!" he commanded, after throwing down his mask next to the amulet.

I knew we weren't far away from where the remaining gauntlets rested. I could feel the power of them, deep in my bones, like a vibration in the marrow. They had rested peacefully for so many centuries without being disturbed. I had to do whatever it took to keep Jason away from them.

Sara and Tabitha had arrived at the entrance to the castle.

"Look, Sara! I see the car!" Tabitha shouted.

Sara parked the van next to the car and jumped out. The doors were unlocked and Sara was able to open the trunk. Still sitting where Eric had placed it, was the duffle bag full of automatic weapons and one of the six gauntlets. The whole time, the two hired thugs had no idea what was right behind them.

"For being ruthless killers, they're not too bright," Sara remarked with a chuckle.

Tabitha unzipped the bag and pulled out two semi-automatic pistols and an assault rifle. She swiftly checked the magazines and loaded them into the guns, before handing them off to Sara. Sara was clearly overwhelmed at the sight of the heavy weaponry. Tabitha did not stop there though, as she found the ancient daggers at the bottom of the bag. Once again, she passed one on to Sara.

"This won't stop them, certainly not all of them, will it?" Sara asked with a hint of dread as she stared down at the ground.

Tabitha carefully slung the assault rifle's strap over Sara shoulder and said with confidence, "Maybe not, but we'll for sure slow them down, hopefully long enough to help Eric."

Tabitha's go-to attitude quickly changed when she noticed the gauntlet was not in the bag. Why take the gauntlet and leave all the weapons? Although a major setback, it was not high on the list of priorities. Staying alive to save Eric was number one.

Sara noticed the sudden change in Tabitha and her heart sank.

"What's wrong?"

"The gauntlet's gone," Tabitha replied.

ETERNAL

"They won't be able to use it, will they?" Sara asked, looking for any sliver of hope.

Tabitha began walking up to the entrance of the castle, "Alex won't be able to use it, but should he get his hands on the others as well, he will finally be able to destroy them all."

In that moment, a courage not of her own, rose up inside of Sara.

"Well then, we better do something about it!" She said, stuffing two grenades inside her coat pocket.

Sara turned and followed Tabitha to the entrance, neither woman affected by the continued onslaught of rain. It didn't take them long to stumble upon the two dead bodies lying in the mud. Sara knelt down next to them, praying that neither one was her husband. She rolled each one over, onto their backs, and was relieved to discover the two men were Eric's captors.

"Who did this?" Sara asked as she picked up her husband's torn shirt in the puddle.

Tabitha did not answer. Deep down, she knew who was responsible and how important it was to reach Eric.

Not too far away, Jason continued to push me onward as fast as he could get me to move, towards the rear of the castle where St. Patrick's Church stood. Cold, wet, and wounded, it took everything I had not to stumble and fall with every step. I could barely see through my swollen eyelids. Jason noticed I was struggling. Like a fellow soldier and friend, he knelt down and hoisted me onto his shoulders. However, this was not to ease my suffering.

It was to ensure I was coherent upon my arrival that would determine my fate.

Propped very uncomfortably over his shoulders, Jason broke into storytelling mode, "A long time ago, before Alex was our leader, the solution to our problem seemed simple. We would just kill the entire bloodline of all of you so-called 'faithful ones'. We succeeded in doing this once, you know. The victory was short lived, however, when we discovered another generation. Another family would be chosen later."

"It was a very costly battle, from what I heard!" Jason exclaimed as he set me on the grass at the back of the roofless church.

After supporting me against a stone wall, Jason concluded his story, "The battle had been so costly in fact, yielding no results, that Alex was placed in charge. His predecessor was banished back to hell, never to return to earth."

I was still tightly bound in handcuffs, my wrists growing evermore bloody from rubbing against the stainless steel. Jason had double checked the cuffs to ensure they were snug. There was no escaping their clutches.

Jason looked down at me, "I would have just killed you and your whole family from the beginning to end this all. You see, I don't really care about this war anymore. It was game over for me the second I decided to go rouge. No member of the fallen has ever just walked away. The others know my plans, there's no escape. But, before I'm cast out, I'll see you and most importantly, Tabitha, dead."

With that, I spoke up, "We all die. It's how I live that matters."

I knew it was a waste of words on a fallen angel that was anything but alive.

Just as the pain was beginning to subside, Jason lifted me up and placed my cuffed hands over the top of a stone gargoyle, located next to the door. I cried out in agony as the cuffs gouged deep into my skin. I was helpless hanging there, nearly three feet off the ground.

The rain continued to fall as the pain kept surging through my body. I tried to grasp the top of the statue in an effort to support my weight. My lack of strength prevented me from doing anything about it though.

Jason stared up into my half-open, wandering eyes, and said, "Now, I know you wouldn't want to miss this beautiful occasion. I'm going to see where the others are. Then, it's curtain call for everyone!"

I began to drift in and out of consciousness. My vision blurred, then abruptly came back into focus. The doubt I felt deep down inside crept to the surface. I wasn't sure if I was going to make it. Was Jason right? An effortless slaughter to end all our hopes?

"I have failed, we have all failed," I said softly to myself as my mind faded deeper into the abyss.

My thoughts now joined with my body to betray the faith I had kept so dear in my heart. I could only hope that Sara would be spared the indignities of our failure.

"Don't give up your faith and sacrifice your loyalties," she had once said.

These devils had no use for Sara, except to use her against me. With everything inside me, I wished something would keep her away from this place of desolation.

My whole body was becoming numb from hanging there for what seemed like hours. All I could feel was the constant beating of rain drops on my neck. This was the only thing keeping me awake at that point.

Then suddenly, through the pelts of rain, a beautiful sound emerged. It was like that of countless angels singing, joined together in unison. I was not alarmed by this, even though I couldn't tell where the sound was coming from. It was faint at first, then grew louder, until it seemed to surround me.

The dark, muddied ground began to slowly illuminate, as if a great light were coming. The sun was still hidden deep behind the clouds. This new light coming towards me was different, special somehow. The singing dissipated as soon as it had begun and only the magnificent light remained.

A gentle voice spoke to me, "Raise up your head, my son."

I mustered all the strength I could and did as the voice asked. I painfully lifted my head from between my arms, which were completely paralyzed. I couldn't believe my eyes, surely I had died and gone to heaven. What I was seeing was not possible. Standing before me was my father, along with three others I did not recognize. An all-consuming light shined behind them.

My father, the great Fredric Richards, walked towards me, he gradually lifted off the ground to meet my gaze.

"I've missed you so much Dad. You made me into the man I am today," I said through tear-filled eyes.

"You have accomplished everything on your own. Your faith has kept you strong.

I am so very proud of you," he replied."

"Proud? Look at where I am! I have failed you all," I said, tears still streaming down my face.

My father put his hand on the side of my face and looked into my eyes.

He smiled and spoke again, "You? Failed? You haven't failed anyone, Eric, look how far you've come! This is not the end. Besides, nothing truly ends. We have been watching over you and we continue to have faith in you."

"I don't think I can do this anymore," I said, looking away from him.

"No one knows what they are capable of until it is required of them. You, my son, are capable of great things."

My father then descended to the ground below me and turned back to look at the others.

"We must go now," he said, walking away from me.

"Wait! Please, don't leave me!" I begged.

"Don't worry, son, we never really leave."

The light then started to fade as my father and the others walked into it. Then, the light quickly disappeared, as did my father.

"Eric!" someone shouted.

I felt my legs being grabbed as my cuffed wrists were lifted off the stone gargoyle.

"Hey! Wake up!" Jason was back, having found his fellow minions, who were eagerly awaiting my arrival.

I laid on the ground, slowly regaining feeling in my limbs. Jason slapped me a few times on the face, in an effort to make me focus on him.

I finally looked up at him and said, "You know, you're done as soon as you show yourself, Jason."

He had the most determined look on his face. It was the look of someone who had nothing to lose. In that moment, I realized just how frighteningly dangerous he really was. He loved killing and enjoyed every gruesome moment of the process.

This time, however, he was on his own. There was no one to pull back on the leash, making him that much more dangerous. You could see only rage and revenge in his blackened eyes. All traces of humanity were long gone in this once normal man. What stood in front of me was simply an empty vessel possessed by a demon.

"You think I would come here without a plan? Eric, you insult me. What I do today will throw a wrench in this entire war! You may as well write it down in God's Eternal Book of Life. This won't end the war, but it will delay the outcome by a couple decades!"

It was no surprise to me that Jason never truly had any interest in the gauntlets. He only wanted to make others suffer, it was like a drug to him. Success for the fallen meant the end of all that. It also meant his very existence would no longer be necessary. I was now at the mercy of this deranged demon.

Jason slowly pulled a radio detonator out of his pocket. Little did I know that he had made a visit to Cashel the night before. He had annihilated everyone in and around the castle, before rigging the whole area with explosives.

The pain from my wounds had miraculously vanished after my father had appeared to me. I had believed it was all a dream, but the absence of hurt from my body proved otherwise. A new found strength seemed to emanate from deep within. I did not show this to Jason, instead continued with the dazed and wounded act.

Jason pulled me up to my feet and began pushing me towards the other side of the church, as I continued to appear weak and vulnerable. Once a vast, royal sea of flowers, the church's garden now stood barren, long since neglected. Alex Reuben and his followers waited in the middle of the plot, adding to the already distasteful scenery. The small army of possessed individuals were emotionless and fully armed.

Before dragging me in front of Alex, Jason whispered in my ear, "Play along or I kill you right here, right now."

What was Jason up to?

Alex looked vastly different, aged at least twenty-five or thirty years. He was far from the dapper forty-year-old millionaire, who stood lying to the masses, taking advantage of his abilities. He had apparently grown weaker, dissolving the energy which had kept up his youthful facade.

He extended his hand, as if this was some kind of friendly invitation. In no way was I about to shake this monster's hand. I knew I would be dead as soon as he had gotten what he wanted.

"Eric, you sure have made things difficult for us," he said in his sly tone.

As Jason handed me over to Alex, I could see his plan beginning to unfold. This was just a waiting game. With a card up his sleeve, Jason would not play it until the timing was right.

At that moment, Jason's plan came to fruition for me. If he could terminate everyone and survive the blast himself, he would be the new leader of the fallen. He would inhabit his rightful position while Alex became a simple casualty. No one would suspect anything, as Alex would be sent back to hell, never to return. Jason's pride began to swell, as his thirst for power overtook him.

I scanned Alex's group of followers. It was obvious he had chosen them at random, civilians from all walks of life. Each one had been seized off the street, while their mental capabilities were immediately surrendered to Alex, who was growing ever-more impatient.

"No more running, no more delays! Show me the gauntlets or die where you stand!" he said with a thundering authority in his voice.

"There is a small problem, Alex. Tabitha has a gauntlet and another is still unaccounted for," Jason interjected, building a false trust with his words.

Jason's statement did nothing to appease Alex.

"I'll deal with you later," Alex said, glaring at Jason.

Alex stared at me with murder in his eyes. There was nothing more I could do to stall the inevitable. Reluctantly, I began walking the two men towards the gauntlets. I could feel their power, it was so great, and it caused me to stumble on first contact. This time, the difficulty walking was not an act, the emanation of divine energy from the gauntlets was nearly breathtaking.

The two possessed men were practically carrying me, as I did my best to fake my weakness. Neither one of them had been affected by the sudden influx of power. The fallen could not feel such a great power.

We had moved towards the base of a tall tower, where inside, a spiral staircase led up to a lookout. Before we could make it inside, we heard a voice that I recognized immediately. It was Sara, the love of my life. I knew she would never leave me.

"Eric!" she cried out, running towards me with Tabitha right next to her.

Alex reacted instantly, commanding his following to kill me. The small army of men and women, absent of all thought, stood like zombies. With his words, they seemed to come to life.

"Run, Sara!" I shouted in a panic.

"Shut up!" Jason scolded me, striking me in the face.

Oddly enough, Jason gave me a half smile, as though his plan had not been altered.

"Enough! Jason, stand guard here, let no one get past you. Prove yourself and I may go easy on your disobedience," Alex said.

The effort to mask what centuries had done to Alex's physical body, was no longer necessary. His face had now significantly aged.

The fire fight started quickly as Sara and Tabitha did not hesitate. Alex's slaves had been armed and wasted no time in putting their weapons to use. The army ranged in age from sixteen to sixty. Even when injured, the possessed pressed on. Driven only to kill, they were not fazed by the impact of a bullet.

The youngest girl charged Sara and Tabitha, showing no sign of fear. Pistol in hand, she headed towards Sara, shooting at the statue she was using for cover. Pieces of stone flew off the statue as Sara did her best to avoid the debris. Tabitha took down as many as she could, buying some time for Sara to recover. Once she did, Sara was still hesitant, only wounding a few. She still saw the army as regular people. Alex knew long before that using everyday civilians would be beneficial for him.

Seeing the struggle in Sara's eyes, Tabitha yelled, "Sara! You have to!"

"I can't!" Sara replied, grimacing with her back to the statue, rifle pointed in the air.

She held tightly on to the gun, trembling as each bullet struck the statue. She had not been in a fight before, nor had we discussed at length her having to kill someday. Unfortunately, the time to kill was now and the mark happened to be a child. If she didn't move past the fact though, they would both die.

This was when I shouted out three words that changed everything, "She's already dead!"

Although not technically dead, the young girl and each follower in Alex's army, would serve the devil the rest of their lives. They might as well be dead. A fully possessed person does not live long, since they are controlled by the lowest form of demon. These beings do not know the human body's need for food, water, or sleep.

My words seemed to sink in. This child was still young enough that her soul would go straight to heaven. I knew Sara all too well to know that she must have been thinking this too. She bowed her head against her AK-47 rifle and began to pray in the midst of the flying bullets.

I could faintly hear her message, "Dear Father, have mercy on these poor souls and let them into your kingdom. Forgive me for sending them on."

Sara then lifted her head, determination shining bright in her eyes. The young girl continued to shoot, even though her gun had run clean out of bullets. Sara seized the opportunity and fired three shots at the girl, two in the chest and one in the neck.

The battle raged on. Two against twenty-five proved too much to handle. Sara had gone down after being shot a number of times, in an attempt to make it to the entrance of the tower Jason was instructed to guard.

Tabitha watched as Sara fell to the ground. She had desperately tried to carry on after sustaining gunshot wounds to the leg and forearm. A lethal blow to her chest ultimately brought her down.

Bleeding severely, she pressed her hand against the center of her chest. The rain diluted the blood and washed it down the stone steps. Summoning all her strength, Sara crawled to the tower and leaned up against the wall.

Enraged, Tabitha threw down her empty pistols and charged the seven remaining dark ones. Her curly, red hair and petite, muscular frame lunged into the air. She raised her gauntlet to the heavens, then landed with great force in the middle of them. Her knuckles cracked as her fist struck the ground, expelling her foes with every drop of water on the grass.

Each one recovered quickly and charged Tabitha with their guns and knives in hand. Tabitha had her hands full, armed with only a dagger. One of the possessed used the chaos as a distraction to somehow slip the gauntlet off of Tabitha's wrist. She was now fighting for her life on her own.

Tabitha pressed on, having no other option except to stand and fight. A punch to her back hindered her deflection of a blade, which cut the palm of her hand. She was relentless though, even pushing through the pain of a gunshot to her shoulder. She continued to eliminate the minions one by one.

"Last one," she thought to herself, doing her best to disregard the pain.

The rain continued to pour as the sun gave way to the thick ominous clouds. In an instant, Tabitha lost her footing and fell to the rain-soaked grass, her own dagger piercing her side. She cried out in agony, certain in her heart, that this would be the end.

Tabitha was in unfamiliar territory, not knowing what to do with a wound that did not heal. Her gauntlet lay in the mud, much too far away to reach. She sat there, grasping her side, and breathing heavy. She nearly passed out, the pain was excruciating, and something she had not felt for decades. She was in a truly vulnerable position as she gazed at the puddle on the ground next to her. Her complexion grew pale, even more so than usual, while her lips turned a slight shade of purple. The rain and cold began to affect her.

On the other side of the courtyard, Sara was still leaning against the wall she had chosen for support. Jason no longer seemed interested in guarding the entrance that Sara was next to. His plan was moving perfectly before him.

Victory was close for Jason McKeenan. Sixty-four years before that very moment, he was insignificant. He was nothing more than a regular man, living his life as a thief.

Leaning over Sara, he was eager to end her life. He lived to kill and eliminating Eric's wife would be especially satisfying. He pressed the barrel of his gun against her temple and was about to pull the trigger when a shout from across the courtyard stopped him.

Tabitha no longer saw killing Jason as revenge for what he had done to her family. It was fate that had carried her to that moment. She saw what Jason was about to do to Sara and let out a blood-curdling scream, the pain evident in her voice. Barely glancing at the only surviving dark one charging towards her, she simply launched her fist into his throat. The man's windpipe was crushed on impact. He clutched at his neck as he collapsed to the ground.

Jason stood laughing at Tabitha, amused by her feeble attempt at fighting back.

"Do you still not see the truth your god has left you? He left you to your own fate because you have failed Him!" he said.

Tabitha gave him no response. Instead, she slowly pulled the blade from her side, gritted her teeth and breathed heavily through the pain. She was not going to die today. It was then that the rain suddenly stopped.

"Come on then!" she yelled back, hobbling to her feet.

Jason charged towards her and with one hand, lifted the tiny redhead off the ground by her neck. Tabitha grasped at her throat, but by some miracle, was able to remain calm.

Before Jason had the chance to end things, Tabitha closed her eyes and placed her left hand on his head.

"See! See the agony and may you go back to hell, holding on to that forever!" she showed him through her memories, those containing the horrific night when he murdered her family.

Jason had fallen into a comatose state and when he came to, Tabitha plunged the dagger, still soaked with her own blood, into his black heart. Jason howled and tossed her into a nearby stone wall, immediately knocking her out cold.

A highly viscous substance began pouring out of Jason's wound. He dropped to the ground, stunned by what had just happened. Laying there in the mud, all he could do was watch the body he had inhabited for so long, be taken away from him. The vessel shriveled before turning a calloused black, as he abandoned it for hell, never to return again.

Tabitha also began to suffer the consequences. Without her gauntlet, she rapidly began aging. The once lively sixteen-year-old was fast approaching the gates of heaven.

Dawning Light

Alex and I were within feet of the remaining gauntlets. He looked back at the entrance to discover that Jason was no longer standing guard and began pulling me towards it. This was when I saw Sara, leaning against the wall, fighting for every breath. I broke Alex's grip and lunged towards my wife.

"Sara, oh God," was all I could say.

Before Alex could stop me from reaching her, a booming voice echoed through the courtyard, "Alex!"

Alex had a look of pure shock on his face. He stared angrily at the stranger, the old man Tabitha and I knew as Father Connolly.

I didn't look away from Sara for one second. My greatest fear had come to fruition, my wife was hurting. She was dying without me being able to ease her suffering.

"It's going to be alright, honey, I will make this better," I told her, as I already knew she was in shock.

"Eric, I'm cold," she whispered through pale lips.

I sat down next to my love and tore the lining out of her jacket and used it to wrap her arm. I pressed my hand against the wound on her chest, in a desperate attempt to stop the bleeding.

Deep down though, I knew the only thing I could do was hold her and comfort her.

I took her in my arms and pulled her jacket up to her neck, trying to make her as warm as possible. The cold was insignificant to me, as tears streamed down my shirtless body.

As I looked down past my wife, I saw what appeared to be a lock at the base of the tower. The shape was familiar. I knew exactly what key would open the stone, as it rested in the mud several yards away, in the form of my necklace. It didn't matter though, the lovely woman in my arms was everything.

Father Connolly picked up Tabitha's gauntlet and brushed the mud and debris off of it. He placed it on her wrist, where it rightfully belonged, and stepped back. Tabitha immediately reverted back to the age of sixteen, although it would take her some time to return to consciousness.

Alex stepped down from the stairs that led to the entrance of the column.

"Who are you?" he shouted at the old man, still dressed in his priestly garb.

The gray-bearded, holy man stood defiant before Alex.

"My name is Liam Connolly, but you may remember me as Jacque de Molay!"

Alex was speechless.

Father Connolly continued, "No longer will I stand by and watch you defile His name!"

The priest rolled up his right sleeve, revealing a gauntlet around his wrist. He looked up to the sky and his eyes shined white for a brief moment.

I was shocked to learn the true identity of the priest. Helpless and unable to come to his aide, I continued to console my wife. I looked up, prepared to beg God for her life, when I saw what was just above us. Jason had planted explosives on the lookout.

Sara seemed to use all her strength to lift her head and gently kiss me. She knew.

"Jason set explosives to kill Alex," I said through tear-filled eyes.

"You know what must be done," Sara whispered back.

She cried and grimaced in pain.

"Honey, I love you. We should pray," I said, not knowing what else I could do for her.

We prayed together, for the safety and guidance of our boys. As we concluded our message and sent our words to heaven, Sara looked up at me in a way I had never seen before. It was a look of fear enveloped in sorrow.

"Will they know, Eric? Will our boys know what happened here?" she asked me.

Through tears of my own I replied, "Yes, my love. The eternal book will show them our journey, through our eyes and thoughts."

I thought of that moment when Anna showed me the book. It had taught me so many valuable lessons, instantly turning a novice into a warrior in this great battle. I hoped Michael would one day find the same book and be guided on a journey of his own.

"Eric, you don't need to be here."

I kissed her and looked up to see the little patch of night sky that was now visible.

"I won't leave you, Sara, and Alex will not reach those gauntlets!"

"Alex, surely you've not lost your memories in your old age?" Molay asked slyly.

The last grand master of the Templar Knights, Jacque de Molay, had been alive after centuries of wearing the gauntlet. The locked tower believed to hold the five remaining gauntlets now only contained four, as Molay had kept the secret for hundreds of years. The body in the tomb believed to be Molay was in fact a devoted follower.

Both men stood before each other. One was the right hand of the devil, while the other was a symbol of faith, who had constructed the gauntlets himself. Alex quickly recognized the man in front of him.

"Why now? After what you did before, why would you stand and fight for them now?" Alex shouted, full of hate and rage.

His right hand began to tremble, the fury rising within. There were too many obstacles in his quest to end the war. He was increasingly losing patience.

"Not for them, but for Him," Molay shouted back.

The old priest, despite having worn the gauntlet for nearly a thousand years, continued to age very slowly.

I didn't want to leave Sara, not even for a second. What would happen next, however, we both knew was unavoidable.

"The detonator is on the other side of the courtyard, in Jason's trench coat," I told her, my eyes spoke volumes, of which I couldn't mask.

"Hold on Sara, we can still make it out," I continued.

"Hurry," she said in between waves of agony.

Relief in the form of numbness overtook her body, combined with the coldness and her blood loss.

Jacque de Molay had his own demons to face and a final battle to wage. In his heart, he knew win or lose, he would not have the strength to continue. This however, did not cause him sadness, instead offered relief. He had one last opportunity to show the Father where his allegiances truly rested.

"Any last words, Jacque Molay the traitor?" Alex bellowed.

As I went to retrieve the detonator, I stopped, weary of the face off that was already in motion. The priest raised his left hand to the sky, revealing what looked like an ancient broad sword. He must have felt my presence, as he glanced over at me.

I somehow heard his voice in my mind say, "Do what you must now. I'll hold him off as long as I can."

The priest then clasped both hands on the sword and shouted, "If He is with me, then who can stand against me?"

Alex and the priest then charged each other.

I had to focus, I needed to find the detonator. Jason's coat laid on the ground. I ran to it and began rifling through the pockets. As I did this, I realized my wife's desire for me to run and be there for our boys. I knew this wasn't an option anymore. I located the detonator and rushed back to Sara, swiping the trench coat on my way.

"Sara!" I cried out, laying the coat on top of her.

Her eyes were closed. I began gently tapping her on the cheek until she finally came to.

"Thank God, you scared me hun."

"I'm so tired," she replied

"Stay with me, it's almost over. Tabitha will be able to heal you."

"No," she said quietly, reaching for the detonator in my hand.

"I'm sorry, Sara, I have to do this," I said, knowing she might not remain awake long enough to flip the switch.

She gazed into my eyes, longingly searching for something. Her complexion was extremely pale, while her lips were a soft blue.

"Eternity waits for us," I told her.

"There's no one else I'd rather share heaven with," she said.

We kissed each other for the last time. I felt her slowly slip away, as her arms, which had been latched onto my shoulders, fell lifeless. The tips of her fingers caressed the ground as they fell. I gently brushed away the loose hair from her face and kissed her forehead.

The tears flowed like a river down my cheeks, "I'll see you soon, Sara."

The fight across from us intensified.

Alex continuously mocked the priest as Father Connolly frantically waved the broad sword in front of him. Alex was still spry, despite his now aged body, and was able to send the priest against a wall with one swift punch.

I sat crouched down in an archway next to the tower, watching history unfold. I took Jason's coat and covered myself in the hopes it would hide my pale, bare chest. The black coat would camouflage in darkness and allow me to execute what needed to be done. This was further fueled by the anger I felt towards my wife's death. Sadness quickly transformed to blazing fire, consuming me like nothing else ever had.

It became evident that although Alex was weakened, the fight still belonged to him. I knew I had become the only obstacle standing between him, a thousand-year-old fallen angel, and his victory. How was I to defeat an evil so powerful?

I watched in disbelief as Alex grabbed the sword from the priest and broke it in two over his knee. Father Connolly retaliated quickly and picked up a stone, slashing Alex's face with a single upward motion. The black sludge that flowed through his veins began to trickle down his diagonal wound.

I knew the priest needed a distraction for Alex to give him the upper hand. I contemplated whether or not I should reveal myself, the only thing I could think of. My hands dug deep into the moist soil, anger rising from within as I stared at Alex. I would have only one shot at what I was about to do. Without the amulet around my neck, there would be no aide from heaven. But, in my heart, I knew I was born to do this, if nothing else.

I stood up and stepped out slowly from behind the tower. The breath in my lungs was heavy as my nerves kept my body in check. Jason's trench coat was still draped over my bruised, shirtless chest. My left hand was in its pocket, clutching the detonator tightly.

"Alex!" I shouted at the top of my lungs.

He quickly turned around, still holding the right side of his face where he had been cut. As I had hoped, the priest seized the opportunity and impaled Alex in the back with his broken sword.

Father Connolly, clothes torn, badly wounded and barely able to stand, was in disbelief as much as I was. Was it possible? Had the great and powerful Alex Reuben been brought to his knees? How could we have ended things in a moment of chance? He cried out in agony as the demon emerged from the old man. For a second, I saw the fallen angel's true form and it was even darker than I could have imagined.

Alex fell to the ground, landing flat on his face, as the half sword still protruded from his back. Black liquid flowed out from underneath his body, encompassing the area around him. The priest walked over to Alex and used his boot to turn him over. The blank stare in his blackened eyes left no doubt.

"We've done it," the priest said, barely loud enough for me to hear.

There was no warning or even a signal, to suggest that Alex would rise from the dead. But he did, as I half expected. He emerged like a twisted phoenix from the ashes of his own lifeless, mortal body. His true demonic form burst forth, shedding its human-like flesh.

The Jacque de Molay, known for six hundred years as Father Connolly would make the ultimate sacrifice. The one who stood as the leader of heaven's resistance on earth, against the fallen, would fall himself. He would be redeemed, however, after centuries of living in shame for his betrayal. This was his greatest act as one of the faithful.

The priest began walking towards me, his back turned to Alex. Shocked and terrified, I had no time to warn him. The black figure oozed from the gash in Alex's chest. The creature pulled the blade out from his back and rose up from the lifeless body.

The first strike took Molay's arm, just below his wrist where the gauntlet rested.

The second motion took his head clean off his shoulders. The priest collapsed to the ground, his head and arm resting several feet away.

Without hesitation, I yelled, "You want me, come and get me!"

By that time, the clouds had dispersed, revealing a clear sky. The brightness illuminated the courtyard like a diamond for the final encounter.

I quickly backed up in shock at the sight of the demon emerging from Alex's shell. The creature forced from its back two wing-like apparatuses. Absent of plush feathers, the wings featured only black skin and bone.

I acted on my first instinct, which was to run back to the tower as the beast began to charge me. Crouched inside the tower, I held the detonator, waiting in anticipation for the right moment.

"God be with me," I said aloud as the demon tried to enter the tower.

The seconds seemed like minutes. Finally, the time came. I flipped the switch. Just as I did, the creature, once known as Alex Reuben, jumped up with its wings spread and launched me against the wall. The remote detonator fell to the floor, although it didn't matter as it failed to activate the explosives.

In a deep, unearthly voice, the demon spoke, "Did you really think that was going to work?"

It motioned towards the charges and began laughing, "I disconnected those before any of you arrived!"

It stepped forward, still mocking me, intent on ending my life.

I did the last thing I could and fell to my knees, "Father, I know you see me..."At this moment, time seemed to stand still, as Tabitha opened her eyes to witness what would happen next.

RISEN

I opened my eyes, unaware of how long I had been unconscious. Everything was blurry at first, but I quickly realized I was still in the courtyard. Pushing through the agonizing headache, I propped myself up against one of the stone pillars.

When my vision cleared, I saw what appeared to be an arm with a gauntlet attached to it. It was Father Connolly's, I knew right away. Eric was across the courtyard from me, a demon-like creature was approaching him as he sought Eric in the tower. I couldn't move, I hurt all over. My only option was to sit there helpless and watch everything unfold.

Suddenly, something happened to Eric. It was difficult to tell, as the beast was blocking my view. Whatever it was, it must have hurt him. He screamed a deep, guttural sound. When the creature finally stepped aside, I clearly saw Eric gripping his sides tightly.

He flung his arms outstretched to the sides of himself, palms facing forward. As he did this, the gauntlet Father Connolly had been wearing, began to move the arm it was still attached to. The arm then slowly lifted off the ground and levitated in the air for a few seconds, before the gauntlet slid off. The disconnected arm fell to the ground while the gauntlet shot over to Eric's arm, as if guided on rails.

Time returned to normal when the gauntlet found his arm. I tried to get as close as I could. It appeared as though the demon was just as surprised as I was. The only difference was that I knew Eric held the capability all along.

"How? You will not steal my victory!" the creature bellowed.

Eric did not acknowledge the threat. His arms were outstretched while his head was tilted back, his eyes looking up. His whole body began to lift up off the ground. He reached three feet, then four, before stopping.

He looked over at me, his eyes slightly glowing white.

His lips did not move, but I heard him still in my mind, "Tell my boys I will always love them. Watch over Michael and don't give up hope for David. I know there is still a chance for him."

With that said, Eric's face began to shine even brighter as he gazed into the heavens. The tower illuminated while the demon could do nothing. Every attempt to reach Eric was met with a jolt that brought the beast to his knees.

As I witnessed the event, I couldn't help but think that there had to be another way. I began to cry, not for Eric, but for his boys. Eric Richards was not the timid, pessimistic disbeliever he once was. In that moment, he had become the most faithful of us all and I would truly miss him.

The entire tower began to shake and the ground trembled around the courtyard. The beast continued, smashing bits and pieces of the stone structure, trying to get inside.

The tower eventually began to crumble, succumbing to the vibrating earth. With a final shout from the creature and a visible smile on Eric's face, the structure collapsed on both of them.

There I was alone amidst the rubble, desperately pulling at the stones. Although my injuries were fully healed, I was still only a sixteen-year-old girl. Many of the rocks were much too heavy for me to move.

Drenched and covered in mud, I grew hysterical. I didn't want to leave Eric and Sara under the debris. This was not going to be their final resting place.

I knew the public could not help. Searching for the Richards' would raise questions that couldn't be answered. The Garda would launch an investigation, the gauntlet would be taken, and the demon would be revealed.

Time was not on my side. Thirty minutes in and I was spent. Before I could go any farther, the angel Anna appeared. She had been quietly watching over and had brought with her a group of other angels. Light shined across the sky as each one descended gracefully to the earth.

Anna didn't say a word, nor did the rest of the heavenly beings. They simply raised their hands in unison, slowly reversing the destruction that had just taken place. I watched as they repaired what had been done with their eyes closed.

Once the tower was reconstructed, Anna and a fellow angel walked inside. As they did, an angel in the courtyard lifted up the body of Jacque de Molay. The angel then walked a few feet and disappeared with Molay into the field. A light shined briefly behind them and they were gone.

I proceeded to follow Anna and the other angel into the tower, but was halted before I could even take two steps. The male angel placed his shining hand on my chest and shook his head, signaling it was best for me not to.

Still upset and confused, I watched as Anna and her fellow spiritual being recovered the bodies of Eric and Sara Richards. Behind them, two more angels carried out a gold case, with what I could only assume, contained the remaining gauntlets.

Through endless tears, I asked, "Where are you taking them?"

"Don't worry, dear Tabitha," Anna said with a solemn look on her face.

Anna knew that was not an acceptable answer for me and continued, "We must find a new place for the gauntlets. Eric, Sara, and Jacque, our three most faithful, will be taken to the temple where they belong."

"The temple?" I asked.

Anna said nothing and walked away with the others.

With complete disregard for any type of respect, I shouted out, "What now? What do I do now?"

Anna looked back and said, "Keep your promise to look after Michael Richards. You will know when to reveal yourself."

Then, she tossed Eric's amulet to me. I stared down at the necklace resting in my hand, then looked over at Eric's lifeless body in Anna's arms.

"Keep that in a safe place for now, along with the Eternal Book, until you think he's ready to know," Anna continued.

After more than sixty years, I had finally seen justice for my family, as Jason McKeenan was finally sent back to hell. It seemed, however, much less gratifying than I had expected. I felt no sense of satisfaction as I had so longed for.

One thing was for sure though. All those who fought dreamed of absolution and an end to all of the bloodshed. It was in that moment that I realized I had been one of the chosen seven all along. Pondering this new revelation, I put my hands in my jacket pockets to keep them warm.

Inside, much to my surprise, was a letter from Father Connolly.

It read, "I know you did not trust me because of the betrayal I once committed. It was during a time when I had lost my way. I'm sorry, Tabitha, I did not tell you who I really was. But know this, we all have a journey. He could have taken Eric here right away to discover the gauntlets. Though, in His wisdom, He knew only the journey would prepare Eric. This is true for you and I as well. However, my travels have come to an end and I leave you with some new knowledge. I sent that young man with the gauntlet your way more than sixty years ago. I knew this was your purpose. May God be with you, my child."

With that, I stood up and walked out of the courtyard. I was all alone, but I knew I would never truly be alone. Eric and Sara would always be with me in spirit. It was the courage he possessed that carried me on. The courage of an ordinary man, called to be a protector, like so many before him. Some grew old, while others like Eric and Sara, gave the ultimate sacrifice for their faith.

The beginning of the last chapter in this eternal fight would soon be written. I did as Anna had said. I returned to New York to break the news to Sara's brother, Arthur.

I gave him the news as softly as I could, along with the personal belongings that the Richards' had with them.

Arthur was silent at the funeral, still frustrated as to why his sister was taken from him. He was told a car accident had been responsible. The most important being that Sara and Eric died together. Michael wept throughout the ceremony. I knelt down and hugged him, intent on keeping my promise to watch over him. As the service concluded, the empty caskets were lowered into the earth.

I did not speak to Michael after that, but instead kept close watch from a distance. I saw so much of his parents in him. I would wait patiently for the day when he too would be ready to carry on his father's legacy. I would open the Eternal Book a few times before returning it. The pages showed me every moment, and it reminded me of how faithful a man Eric was.

I knew deep in my heart, that one day, we would win this war. The fallen would see our determination and face our resistance!

In the weeks, months, and years that followed, I would often return to that place, the Rock of Cashel. I'd think about the love that Eric and Sara shared. Even with insurmountable odds, they stood together. Without any special gift, power, or call to fight, she stayed by his side.

It had never been her battle to wage. But yet, without Sara beside him, would Eric have done what was needed?

A light, not usual to the sun, shined through as I walked, sipping on my tea, along the castle wall. I felt the two of them, and watching the light, I knew it must have been coming from them. It brought reassurance and a smile to my face.

Feeling euphoria in that ancient place, little did I know what was happening miles away. Michael's twin brother, David, was being presented to the legion of fallen souls. Just eight years old, he was beginning his own chapter.

"Is he ready, Carter?" a blonde-haired, tall, possessed man in uniform asked.

"Yes, he is dressed."

Carter escorted the young boy, who was chosen to lead the devil's legion, down the long hallway. As soon as he reached maturity, David would be their savior.

They walked to the balcony together, then Carter raised his hand up and shouted, "The chosen, David Richards! Long live the chosen!"

The masses gathered below, joined Carter, and chanted in unison, "Long live the chosen!"

ABOUT THE AUTHOR

 David Gere had a dream in 1996 that would be the inspiration for this story ten years later. He spent the majority of his early years in New York and Oregon, before making his home in Washington State. After a difficult upbringing, he found triumph in studying theology and conducting ministry work. His experiences living abroad in Ireland gave him the motivation to complete this tale.

Follow the Eternal Saga at:
www.theeternalsaga.com